I0761764

THE DANCE OF DEATH

To save the one she loves, she'll kill them all.

Kiku's quest to rescue her lover has gone disastrously wrong. With the odds stacked against her, her enemies think she'll run and hide to save herself. They're wrong—dead wrong. Kiku decides to take the fight to them instead. Now the hunter, Kiku, will stop at nothing to protect those she loves.

WARNING: If you have plans, cancel them! Call in sick to work, get a babysitter, do whatever you must to steal away with Kiku. You won't be able to stop reading, so get ready to strap in, buckle up, and hang on for the action-thrill ride of your life!

Praise for Christopher Greyson's
The Dance of Death

A winner!

I loved every minute of it!

Move over Bond, here comes Kiku!

If you like Mission Impossible, you will love Kiku!

This book is so action-packed I had to remind myself to breathe!

A truly fun and face-paced read! Kiku is a kick-butt action hero, but her character is balanced by a vulnerability that adds depth and complexity.

From multi-award-winning *Wall Street Journal* bestselling author Christopher Greyson comes this spellbinding tale with jaw-dropping secrets, a colorful ensemble of characters, and a protagonist you'll root for from the first page to the last. Christopher Greyson's novels have been read by millions of readers.

ALSO BY CHRISTOPHER GREYSON

The Girl Who Lived

One Little Lie

Pure of Heart

The Adventures of Finn and Annie

The Detective Jack Stratton Mystery-Thriller Series:

And Then She Was Gone

Girl Jacked

Jack Knifed

Jacks are Wild

Jack and the Giant Killer

Data Jack

Jack of Hearts

Jack Frost

Jack of Diamonds

Captain Jack

Kiku - The Yakuza War Trilogy

A Beautiful Place to Die

Kindle the Fires of War

Dance of Death

This book is dedicated to my martial arts instructor-Mark Ricci. He poured titanium into my spine and showed me how to walk as both a warrior and kind man.

The Dance of Death

WALL STREET JOURNAL BESTSELLING AUTHOR

CHRISTOPHER GREYSON

GREYSON MEDIA

1

Kiku's eyes snapped open, to a world of pure black and freezing cold. She shivered as her confusion grew. She was certain her sins had earned her a VIP ticket into Hell. She had always expected to face roaring flames when she died. Which left her wondering where the fire was. *Is this what Hell is really like? Cold, dark, solitary?*

Vivid flashes of her last conscious recollections played one after the other like a sick slide show: Takeo's shirt turning crimson; her hand pressed against his gunshot wound; Dr. Ito in the morgue. Then ...

Like the blast of a gun, the name of her mentor roared in her mind. *Daichi.* His face filled the screen in her head, and his words of betrayal echoed like thunder: "Jiro offered me a job."

Forcing herself to focus, Kiku fought back the hot brew of feelings that boiled up with these memories. Like a sailor after a wild night of leave, she racked her clouded mind to recall crucial information locked within.

The slide show of her last moments before death resumed. She had given Takeo so much of her blood that she was about to pass out when Daichi came into the morgue and attacked her. In her weakest moment, he had killed her.

Kiku willed herself to think about what had almost certainly happened next. Takeo, too, had been near death on the table beside her when Daichi smothered her.

Snuffed out like a candle—instead of the fight to the death she had always envisioned for herself. She shivered and wondered again what this cold world was—perhaps a special hell for assassins. In which case, Daichi might be here with her now.

Kiku smiled in the darkness. If he *was* here, things were about to get a lot worse for him, but a lot more interesting for her.

She tried to sit up, but after rising only four inches, her forehead banged into metal above her. Her head dropped back down, striking the metal slab beneath her. She reached out her hands on each side, and her fingers touched cold steel.

She tried to calm her breathing as her hands explored the surfaces of the metal box she was trapped in. She felt no latches, no handles. She inched her way down until her feet touched the end of the box and tapped it a few times, trying to gauge its strength. Then she kicked it as hard as she could. A deafening noise reverberated through the box, like she was inside a steel barrel that was being used as a drum.

She had just raised her leg to kick again when she felt herself sliding backward, being pulled from the box like a knife from a kitchen drawer. She had to blink against the suddenly blinding lights, but she recognized where she was: the morgue. She had been placed feet first into one of the refrigerators used to store the dead.

Daichi appeared at her side and glared down at her.

Kiku ripped the gun from his waistband and aimed it at his groin. "Move and you die." She could barely see, but she resisted the temptation to wipe her eyes. "Hands on top of your head."

"Hand." Daichi corrected her, flashing the roguish grin he was famous for. "And can you please point that thing someplace else?"

"Where is Takeo?"

"Kiku, you need to take it slow, but we don't have a lot of time. I—"

"Shut up. You betrayed us."

"What are you talking about?"

"You said you are working for Jiro."

"I think the doc took too much blood out of you and it shriveled your brain." Daichi laughed.

Kiku jabbed the gun into his stomach. "You tried to kill me."

Daichi scowled. "I don't *try* to kill people, I *do* kill them. And I don't return to check if they're all right, either."

Kiku shook her head like a swimmer trying to get water out of her ears. What he said was true, but ...

"Why did you smother me?"

"The cops were coming. Don't forget, we're in the basement of the police station, and I needed to hide you. The only option was to stick you in the drawer. But you were so out of it, I couldn't instruct you to be quiet, and I was afraid you were going to make too much noise. I had to knock you out somehow. Would you have preferred I punch you in the head?"

As a matter of fact, she *would* have preferred a quick punch to the head, but now she understood his motivations.

"Okay." She lowered her gun and tried to sit up.

Daichi grabbed her arm and pulled her to a sitting position.

"Where is Takeo?" Kiku asked.

Daichi's face fell. "Dead."

Kiku didn't cry out. She didn't shed a tear. Her emotions, suddenly so cold, they burned.

When her icy stare met Daichi's, the veteran hitman's eyes widened in fear, and he stepped back.

Kiku slid off the table. "Let me see his body."

"That's not possible—"

"Now!" Kiku growled.

Daichi sighed. "Okay." He held up both hands. "Takeo's not exactly dead—yet."

Kiku grabbed Daichi's shirt and placed the gun barrel beneath his chin.

"Will you stop doing that?" Daichi said. "You're shaking so bad that gun's going to go off."

"Why would you lie to me about Takeo?"

"Because I want to keep you both alive. If you thought Takeo was dead, you'd agree to let Dr. Ito sneak you out of here. But if you knew Takeo was alive, you'd insist on coming with me."

She lowered the gun. "Since when is that a bad idea?"

"Ordinarily, you're the best asset in any arsenal, but right now there's an army of cops and Yakuza across the street, and they all want us dead. I'm going to have to run the gauntlet, and I'm going to have to move fast. You can barely stand."

"I am coming with you." Her legs shook as she walked over to the coat rack, took down a white lab coat, and put it on.

"Look at you!" Daichi rubbed his forehead with his good hand. "That's why I lied. You're going to slow me down, and I don't have time to wait for you to recover. The cops are about to bring a lot of bodies in here."

"I know." Kiku buttoned her coat. "I am the one who killed them. Where is Takeo?"

"In a hearse outside."

"You left Takeo outside?"

"No one's going to be looking in there," Daichi said. "He's in a coffin. Besides, he's been out there this long because you're holding me up."

"I am ready." Kiku strode down the hall, forcing Daichi to catch up with her. But she stopped after opening the door to the outside, stunned by the police lights and razzle-dazzle of numerous news crews. But what really caught her eye was the decked-out Japanese hearse parked just outside the doors. Every Japanese person secretly longed to be conveyed to the afterworld in such a hearse. Onto the body of a limousine was grafted a fanciful Buddhist temple carved out of wood and painted gold, black, and red, and a grinning golden dragon ran along the entire roof. Suddenly, Kiku wondered again if Daichi had killed her and this was some hallucination from the afterlife. She was dead, Takeo was dead—

She swayed and Daichi caught her arm, looking at her with concern. "Are you all right, Ōkami? We must hurry."

Feeling his powerful muscles and hearing his old nickname for her woke her up to the real world, and reminded her that in order to survive, she must be like the tough little native wolf for which she was named. She took a deep breath and readied herself for battle. She nodded to Daichi, quickening her pace toward the otherworldly chariot that held her lover, clinging to life. She did not allow herself to look at the coffin in the back, for she'd want to climb in with him.

"Does he have enough air?" she asked as she buckled herself in.

"He's on oxygen. But we need to get him to a doctor fast." Daichi pulled away from the morgue, but because of the scene they were fleeing—which they had caused—the police had set up a roadblock. A young policeman approached Daichi's window.

Daichi jerked his thumb toward the coffin in the back. "We have orders to move some of the bodies already processed to make more room."

The policeman glanced down at Daichi's lab coat. "Where's your badge?"

"My regular lab coat got covered in, ah ... intestinal fluid." Daichi shrugged. "I grabbed a clean one, because you don't want to be walking around like that. You know what I mean?"

An older cop shouted, "What's the holdup?"

Kiku's heartbeat was ticking up. She felt nauseated, and it was getting worse.

"He doesn't have a badge," the young one shouted back.

The older policeman rolled his eyes. "Look around, rookie. Let 'em go."

Daichi nodded vigorously. "Thank you." He started to roll forward, but the policeman's hand came down on the windshield.

"Hold on." The rookie peered across the seat at Kiku. "Let me see *your* badge."

She smiled apologetically. "They just called me in. I was shopping with my husband and came right over."

"Officer Tanaka!" the old cop bellowed.

The muscles in the young cop's jaw flexed. Kiku recognized his look of resolve. He was going to follow procedure no matter what his superior wanted. He was going to order Daichi to get out of the car. Daichi must have picked up on the expression too, because he jammed his foot down on the gas.

The hearse smashed through the sawhorses and shot through a gap in the line of police vehicles, as every cop with a gun opened fire. Bullets pinged off the hearse as Daichi raced across the mall parking lot.

In her side mirror, Kiku saw policemen rushing to their cars. "Here they come," she said.

Daichi swore and turned the steering wheel hard to the right. The hearse slid into the curve toward the mall exit. "This is like riding a pig with a fat butt."

Kiku laughed. Maybe it was due to loss of blood or the depths of her exhaustion, but the thought of Daichi galloping down the streets of Sendai on the back of a pig made her laugh so hard her sides hurt.

As he exited the mall and lumbered onto the main road, Daichi gripped the wheel with his prosthetic hand and fumbled for his phone with the other. "Kiku, can you grab my phone from my shirt pocket?"

She grabbed the phone. "What is the passcode?"

"One-one-one-one," Daichi said as he swerved around a truck.

Kiku chuckled. "Simpleton."

"Shut up. You try unlocking a phone with one hand. Speed-dial four and hold the phone to my ear."

"Left!" Kiku shouted.

A car had stopped at a red light directly in front of them.

Daichi cut the wheel right and struck the curb. The limousine leapt into the air so hard both their heads hit the headliner. The car crashed back down with sparks flying up behind them.

"I said left!" Kiku growled as she held the phone against Daichi's ear.

"Hello?" Daichi shouted into the phone. "Everything's gone south. I'm heading for downtown."

Kiku heard a man's voice through the tiny speaker. "You're heading south?"

"No!" Daichi pumped the brakes, cut the wheel, and slid around a turn. "I'm in the hearse, headed *north* to the business district. The cops are after us. Where's the other ride?"

The man replied, but this time Kiku couldn't make out his words. As Daichi ran a red light, he flashed his roguish grin. "I still have some friends in Japan."

Kiku returned the phone to his pocket and was watching a line of police cars now stretched out behind them in her side mirror when a bullet struck it, shattering the glass.

"Why are they shooting?" Kiku asked, puzzled. Japanese police procedure mandated that officers were not to shoot during chases.

"Kenzo's men ran into the cops when they were escaping from the mall. Dozens of policemen were killed in the resulting firefight."

Kiku clenched her jaw. That would certainly complicate matters. "Do you have a plan?"

Daichi smiled. "Hang on. You might not like this part." He cut the wheel and headed for a grassy slope that led up to the interstate.

"I thought we were going to the business district."

"We are. I'm just opening up some space between us and the police."

The engine whined, and the tires spat out chunks of turf. At the top of the hill, the hearse crashed through a chain-link fence and then they were airborne, flying across the highway. Horns blared, tires skidded, and a huge truck almost tore them in half as the oncoming vehicles tried to avoid the crazed golden dragon.

Kiku felt vomit rising in her throat. She turned her head and threw up out the window just before the car came back to earth with surprising grace. Daichi spun the wheel and took off down the highway.

Wiping her mouth with the back of her hand, Kiku glanced back. "We still have three cruisers in pursuit." She could only hope that Takeo was well cushioned in his casket, and still unconscious.

"Not for long." Daichi pointed. Just up ahead, an older man stood beside a truck at the side of the highway. He was holding a cable, and stop sticks were stretched across the road. As soon as the hearse had passed over them, the man yanked the cable.

The pursuing police cars skidded in an effort to avoid the metal spikes. But they couldn't stop quickly enough. The tires on all three cruisers were shredded.

Daichi barreled off the highway and into the business district. He didn't slow until he skidded to nearly a full stop and turned sharply down an alley. A florist's truck sat idling behind a restaurant, its cab facing them. Daichi pulled around the truck and backed up to it. When five men ran out the back door, Kiku pulled her gun, but Daichi placed a restraining hand on her arm. "They're with me."

As he got out of the car and removed his white coat, the men ran to the back of the hearse and lifted the coffin out. They quickly loaded it into the back of the truck, strapped it down, and hid it underneath boxes of flowers, then filed back into the restaurant without having uttered a word.

Daichi helped Kiku out of the hearse and took off her lab coat as well. Then he put an arm around her and half-supported her to the passenger side of the flower truck. The world was spinning beneath her, and walking the few steps to the truck was like crossing a ship's deck in the midst of a storm.

He opened the cab door. "You get the window seat. I don't want you puking on me." He slid into the middle of the cab, pulled Kiku in beside him, and reached over her to shut the door.

The engine rumbled to life, and Kiku turned to look at the driver. When she saw who it was, she drew her gun, reached across Daichi, and pressed it against the driver's temple.

Jimmy raised his trembling hands from the steering wheel. "Please don't shoot my brains out. I can explain."

2

"I can explain," Jimmy repeated.

Kiku kept the gun pressed against his temple. "You can try."

Daichi glanced in the side mirrors. "We need to leave."

"Let him explain first," Kiku said sternly, leaving no room for debate.

Jimmy smiled awkwardly. "I'm a moron?"

"Good enough for me. Hit the clutch, Jimmy." Daichi pushed down on the gas and shifted the gear while Jimmy's foot was on the clutch. "I did that with my prosthetic," he announced proudly.

Kiku did not lower her gun.

"Can you at least wait to shoot him?" Daichi asked as he steered with his good hand.

"Hey! Don't say that!" Jimmy's eyes widened as they started moving down the alley.

"I'm trying to reach a compromise," Daichi explained.

"A better compromise is to say, forgive him and let it go," Jimmy said hopefully. He started to reach for the steering wheel and Kiku's eyes narrowed.

"Put the gun down, Kiku. We're reaching the main street. Clutch!" Daichi switched gears again. "You can shoot him when we get where we're going, okay?"

"Will you *stop* saying that?" Jimmy shrieked. "You don't know her. She'll shoot me right now."

Daichi grinned broadly. "Keep driving. Nobody knows Kiku like I do. And she won't shoot you now because she knows if she shot you, we'd have blood all over the windshield, which would make it hard for us to drive around Sendai without drawing attention. And we need to get Takeo to the doctor as fast as possible." He looked at Kiku. "Right?"

Jimmy looked like he was starting to hyperventilate, but he kept driving. The truck sped up as they reached the main street. Daichi went to switch gears and Jimmy grabbed his prosthetic and then let go like he'd grabbed a snake.

"I got it now," Jimmy said.

Daichi sat back in his seat. "I was starting to get the hang of it."

"He betrayed us," Kiku snarled. "I will shoot him low down. We can stuff his body at my feet. You can drive."

"*Jiro* betrayed us," Daichi said. "Not Jimmy." He pressed Kiku's gun arm down, the muscles in his forearm straining. "You are strong, Ōkami. Even when you are ready to pass out."

"Do not change the subject. He led Takeo into a trap."

"I didn't—" Jimmy started to say.

Kiku dropped the gun into her lap, grabbed it with her other hand, and aimed it at Jimmy's head.

Daichi placed his prosthetic hand in front of the barrel, blocking it.

Kiku glared at him. "That is cheating."

Daichi winked.

"I don't know if that will stop a bullet," Jimmy said nervously. He pressed himself back into the seat as if he could hide behind Daichi.

"No time like the present to find out," Kiku said calmly.

Daichi tilted his head toward the road. "Kiku. Cops."

With a scowl, Kiku lowered her gun as two cruisers sped past, likely en route to the mall.

"Yamagata police. They're calling in cops from all over," Daichi said. "Kiku, please. Drop this until we get Takeo someplace safe."

Reluctantly, Kiku nodded.

Jimmy exhaled.

Daichi pulled a plastic bag from his pants pocket and handed it to

Kiku. "Eat these. Baba made them. They are crumbled, but good." He smiled and patted his stomach.

Kiku nibbled the peanut-butter cookies as they rode in silence, the business district gradually giving way to residential housing and family neighborhoods.

Daichi's phone rang. He listened for a moment, thanked the caller, and hung up.

"The police have set up a perimeter around the entire city," he said. "But there's no need for us to worry. We're almost there."

Jimmy stopped the truck in front of a modest two-story house and backed into the driveway.

Waiting for them outside was a middle-aged woman, thin, with blond hair.

"Her name's Olivia," Daichi said to Kiku as they all got out of the truck. "She can be trusted."

Jimmy opened the rear of the truck, and Olivia and Daichi climbed inside. They moved the flower boxes covering the coffin, then removed the straps holding it in place.

Olivia started to open the lid, but Daichi shook his head and put a hand on her arm.

"I should check if he can be moved," Olivia said.

"He doesn't have a choice. We've got to get rid of this truck."

Olivia nodded and helped Daichi push the coffin to the end of the truck. Kiku and Jimmy grabbed the end, pulled it to the edge, and waited for Olivia and Daichi to jump down and join them. Like four pallbearers, they carried the coffin down a little walkway to the rear of the house. Kiku knew Jimmy was bearing most of the weight of their end. She was having a hard enough time just walking and was doing little more than balance her side of the coffin.

As they awkwardly stumbled into the house, Olivia grunted, "To the right."

Kiku's arms shook as they set the coffin down in a living room that had been converted into a makeshift hospital room and filled with medical equipment. Daichi looked around and nodded approvingly.

"Let's get to work," Olivia said, lifting the coffin lid.

Kiku moved closer. When she saw Takeo, her knees buckled, and she grabbed the doorframe for support. He looked dead. His face was gray, splattered with blood, and frozen in pain. The oxygen tube had come out of his mouth, probably early in the ride when they flew across the highway. She watched until she saw his chest rise.

There's still hope.

Olivia bent over him and examined his wound. After a minute, she stood up. "The doctor who treated him was smart—he placed a backboard beneath him. Help me get him onto the bed."

The four of them maneuvered Takeo onto the hospital bed. He groaned weakly as they removed the backboard, but his eyes remained closed.

"I need everyone to leave the room, please." Olivia pointed to the door.

"Just one moment, please." Kiku approached Takeo, took his hand in hers, and gently squeezed it as she whispered into his ear.

Takeo didn't respond.

A tear dared to splash from Kiku's eye, but she annihilated it before it could land on her cheek. "*Domo arigato*, Olivia," she said as she turned and headed out.

Daichi led Kiku and Jimmy down a short hallway to the kitchen.

Jimmy leaned against the counter and said, "Now what?" as casually as if he were asking how to operate the coffeemaker.

Kiku reached for her gun, growling, "Now you explain how you betrayed us." But her holster was empty. With a glare at Daichi, she grabbed a chef's knife from the butcher block on the counter.

"Kiku!" Daichi leapt between her and Jimmy.

"I said I'm sorry!" Jimmy, now trapped between Daichi and the counter, pled his case: "I swear I didn't know!"

"Look, Kiku, I can explain everything," Daichi said. He pointed to a chair at the kitchen table. "Let me make you a cup of tea and we can discuss this."

"I would love a cup of tea, thank you. Right after I kill this treasonous rat."

"How about you kill him after he moves the truck?" Daichi said. He slowly circled around Kiku, pulling Jimmy behind him.

"Can you stop telling her to wait to kill me and just tell her *not* to kill me?" Jimmy said, ducking low behind Daichi. "I swear—"

"If you deny it one more time, I *will* cut your heart out."

"I'm sorry!"

"Shut up and move the truck!" Daichi ordered as he backed Jimmy toward the door. "You do know that Kiku is an expert at throwing knives?"

Jimmy sprinted out the door.

Daichi exhaled. "Now, Kiku, will you please sit down?"

She slammed the knife back into the butcher block.

Jimmy poked his head around the doorframe. "How am I getting back?"

"Walk!" Daichi snapped.

"It's ten miles!"

"Are you in a hurry to get back and talk to Kiku?"

Kiku ripped the gun from Daichi's waistband, and Jimmy vanished from sight. Running footsteps and a slamming door announced his wise departure.

"Give me that!" Daichi pulled the gun from her hand. "Now sit down!"

Kiku, normally so graceful, felt as if she had no control over her muscles as she weakly flopped down on a chair and placed her elbow on the table. "You have gone soft. Your nephew could die because of him—and your great-nephew, too, if he told Jiro that Alex is alive."

Both stopped talking at the mention of Takeo's young son, Alex. He was in hiding on Daichi's farm and safe for now.

"That was the first thing I made sure of. Had Jimmy revealed the truth about Alex, I would've killed him already myself. Jimmy thought he was doing the right thing. Jiro told him he was trying to get Kenzo and Takeo to reach a truce. Jiro played him, Kiku, the same way he played you."

Kiku's eyes narrowed.

Daichi calmly walked over to the stove, picked up the teakettle, and filled it with water. "He played me, too. At first."

"How did he even find you?"

"He didn't. I found him. I heard what happened with you three in Russia."

"Because Jimmy told Jiro we were taking the cruise! Otherwise, we would have made it to Alaska. And I bet the Russians found us on the train because of him, too."

"Jimmy's a moron. We've established that." Daichi put the kettle on the stove. "But he had good intentions."

"The road to Hell is paved with good intentions. Now tell me how Jiro played you."

Daichi frowned. "He thanked me up and down. He was so grateful for my help. Told me I was like a father to him. But once I got here, he revealed his grand scheme to take over the Yakuza. He figured I would side with him against Kenzo, given what Kenzo had done to me. I tried to talk Jiro out of it, but it was too late."

"How did you find us?"

"Jiro told me of the meetup in Sendai, and I found Jimmy. He kept watch on you as you went into the mall, then saw you exit to the morgue. He even took out a couple of Kenzo's men on your tail."

"Do not expect me to thank him for that. He drew us into their crosshairs."

Daichi leaned against the counter and crossed his arms. "No. Jiro is to blame. His plan was brilliant. He lured all his enemies into one trap —Kenzo, Takeo, you—figuring you'd all kill each other and whoever was left would get swept up by the police next door. Jimmy was trying to be loyal."

Kiku scowled—because Daichi was right. The plan *was* superb. When she saw Jiro next, she'd have to make sure to compliment him. Right before she put a bullet in his head.

"What I don't understand," Daichi continued, "is why Kenzo had Takeo shot. My brother has an obsession with his lineage."

Guilt washed over Kiku. She bent forward, one hand wrapping around her stomach. "That was my fault. I missed it." She rubbed her eyes with the heel of her hand. They were watering and getting worse. It must be a side effect from giving so much blood.

It couldn't be tears. She never cried. Never.

"You missed what?" Daichi asked.

"When Takeo was in Fumeiyo no ie, Kenzo ordered a prostitute to lie with Takeo. He wanted her to collect Takeo's seed—to make an heir. I ... I was that prostitute. Or at least, I acted as one, in order to gain entrance. But to make our escape, I had to give them what they wanted. I needed to stall them ..."

"Good intentions," Daichi said softly.

Kiku ground her teeth. "Kenzo must have greatly loved Takeo's mother," she said, "to be so insistent on having an heir born of her line."

"Love?" Daichi scoffed. "Kenzo loves himself. Always has, always will. He didn't love Itsumi, he was obsessed with her. He killed her fiancé. Tortured the guy for three days to find out all about Itsumi. All her secrets. He eventually married her, but when she didn't produce an heir ... he beat her so bad I thought he'd kill her." Daichi's hand balled into a fist. "It wasn't because of Itsumi she couldn't get pregnant. The great Kenzo is impotent. He won't admit it, so he blamed her. He did the same thing to Jiro's mother when she didn't get pregnant."

"How did Itsumi die?" Kiku leaned her head into the palm of her hand. She was so tired.

"Drowned. She went swimming in their pool. No one asked why she would go swimming so late in the year on such a cold night. Maybe because no one but Kenzo and I knew that Itsumi was afraid of the water."

Kiku's eyelids felt so heavy. "He killed her ..."

Daichi shrugged. "My brother is an evil man." The teakettle whistled, and he took it off the burner. "He picked Itsumi because she was gorgeous and graceful, and he thought she would provide an heir worthy of him. And once she had done that ... he no longer had need of her. What he never realized was that she was even more beautiful on the inside."

Kiku's head sagged forward and dropped off her hand. "I have to fix my mistake. We need to get that vial back."

She tried to sit up straight, but her body wasn't cooperating. She felt herself sliding off the chair. Daichi was suddenly at her side and he scooped her up in his arms.

She shook her head. "No, no bed, get the vial ... If Kenzo ... Buy time. Kill them all."

Daichi carried her into a sitting room and laid her gently on a couch. It was so soft, Kiku felt like she was being swallowed by it. She closed her eyes. A blanket was laid over her, and her cold body sucked up its warmth.

Daichi's fingertips brushed her dark hair off her pale face. He leaned close to her. She could feel his breath on her cheek. "I'll fix everything. Good night, Ōkami."

3

With its metallic sign and techno swirled logo, the ultramodern building looked like the office of some tech company. But it was actually a fertility clinic that, for the right price, would give you whatever baby your heart desired—no questions asked.

"They've got a lot of security," Daichi noted, as relaxed and calm in the passenger seat as if they were buying groceries back in the States, where no one knew who he really was. Yet they were in Japan, where hundreds of enemies wanted him dead.

Kiku held up her phone and scrolled through photographs of the higher-ranking doctors. "Keep watching for any of these men exiting the building."

Daichi pointed to a picture. "That guy was pulling out in a blue BMW when we arrived."

Kiku frowned. "Dr. Sugawara. Head of research. He would have been perfect if you had mentioned it at the time."

"He was already leaving, and you hadn't even shown me the photos yet. Wait! What about him?" Daichi pointed to a tall man with graying hair who was heading for a shiny new Lexus.

"Dr. Mori Sano." Kiku scrolled back to his picture. "Jackpot. Head of fertility." She put the car in drive and followed the Lexus out of the parking lot. As she drove, she typed a text with one hand. *Please get me all information on Dr. Mori Sano—Sendai, Japan. TY.*

"Who are you reaching out to?"

"A friend in the states. Alice is a private investigator and computer whiz. She can find anyone."

Daichi tipped his own phone up, checking the screen.

"Any updates?" Kiku asked.

Daichi grimaced. "Olivia says Takeo's not bleeding, but ... he's burning up. She's sure Dr. Ito removed the bullet, but she thinks the wound is infected."

"The man shot through his jacket pocket." Kiku's fingers tightened around the steering wheel as she replayed the event in her mind. "The bullet could have deposited fabric from his jacket, or from Takeo's own shirt." She slowed down to let a car pull between her and the Lexus.

"Or the infection could be from doing the surgery in a morgue."

"Is Takeo receiving antibiotics?"

"Jimmy's working on it."

"*Working* on it? Takeo needs them *now*!"

"Ease up. You can't just get them at the pharmacy. Jimmy's been working nonstop procuring stuff, and if you keep pressing him, you're only going to make him screw up and get us all caught. Did you know he was going to sleep out in the car last night?"

"He should be happy I am allowing him to draw breath, let alone sleep in a comfortable bed."

"You should be happy that I convinced him *not* to sleep in the car. If a neighbor saw him, they'd call the cops. You'd kill the cops, and you'd keep killing them until they killed you. Then they'd take Takeo to a hospital, where Kenzo would find him and kill him. So either you let this thing with Jimmy go, or *you* are going to get Takeo killed. Got that?"

"If you would just let me kill Jimmy, that would also solve the problem."

"Jimmy screwed up. He's apologized, and he's working hard to make amends. What will it take for you to let it go?"

Kiku ignored the question. Whether out of stupidity, misguided loyalty, or evil intent, Jimmy had betrayed them. She had no intention of letting it go.

Dr. Sano's Lexus pulled onto the interstate. Kiku stayed a few cars behind him. After they had driven in silence for several minutes, Kiku's phone vibrated with a text. She glanced at the screen, then summarized: "Dr. Sano lives alone. Twice divorced. No children." She typed back: *Thank you. Sorry to disturb you while you are planning your wedding.*

Daichi checked his own phone, then began tapping his prosthetic on the door.

"Are you expecting a call?" Kiku asked.

"Jiro."

Kiku sat up straight. "Why is he calling you?"

"He thinks Jimmy and I are working for him."

"Have you spoken with him?"

"Of course. I told him that I am scouring hospitals and clinics looking for you and Takeo, and Jimmy is checking with his connections."

Kiku let her right hand relax into her lap. "Why did you keep this fact from me?"

"Well, you haven't been your usual ray of sunshine lately. You're ready to shoot anyone who looks sideways at you. Even more so than usual." Daichi shook his head. "Someday you'll have to really trust someone."

"I just tried that. It did not work out so well." Kiku slowed down and changed lanes. "Maybe I do not trust you because you are giving me cause not to. Think about it. It is very fortunate that the fertility clinic Kenzo sent Takeo's sample to just happens to be in Sendai."

"That's no coincidence. Jiro knew where his dad was, and Kenzo wanted to personally oversee the process. That's why Jiro picked Sendai for the meetup." Daichi leaned against the door, his jawline hardening. "There's nothing suspicious about it, and if you were on top of your game, you'd see that."

Kiku nodded, though she bristled at the slight. The silver Lexus exited the highway, and she followed at a respectable distance.

"You could start by trusting me, you know," Daichi said. "How long have we known each other?"

"Too long. And what about the time you shot me?"

Daichi shook his head. "I wasn't trying to kill you, but I had to make it look good."

"You made it look *too* good. I thought you were serious."

"A mistake I will never forget." He held up his prosthetic hand.

Kiku forced the memory of that day out of her mind to concentrate on her present task. Her phone buzzed with another message from Alice, and she glanced at it.

"Well?" Daichi asked.

"The doctor has no girlfriend and is not seeing anyone so far as my friend can find. I say we hit him after he shuts off the alarm but before he gets settled. Here." She handed him her phone.

"What am I looking at?"

"Google satellite images of the doctor's house."

"Your friend is good." Daichi pointed at the picture. "This driveway is long and runs down next to this road. The trees would give me cover. Drop me off and I'll see if I can slip into the garage after him."

Kiku nodded. "I will wait five minutes and then drive down and go to the front door. Agreed?"

"Agreed."

When Dr. Sano turned onto the road next to his street, Kiku pulled over and Daichi jumped out. Without a word, Kiku hit the gas and started after Dr. Sano again. Alice was the best researcher she'd ever met, but things could go wrong. Who knew if the doctor had moved or if the address on the Internet was wrong?

But Alice had been correct. The doctor turned down the long driveway. Kiku cruised to a stop and checked her phone like she was looking for directions. She went so far as doing a reverse address search on Dr. Sano's neighbors to use as a cover in case the police showed up.

After waiting five minutes, she restarted the car and drove up the driveway. The doctor's large cabin-like home was isolated, set far back from the road and away from the neighbors. No one would hear someone screaming inside if the windows were shut.

As she parked, she scanned the woods near the garage, but didn't see Daichi. That was good—odds were he was inside the garage. She got out, strolled up to the door, and rang the doorbell.

Dr. Sano answered the door with the chain still attached. He peered through the crack and eyed Kiku suspiciously. "Yes?"

Kiku smiled warmly. "I'm so sorry. I'm looking for Sumi Tanaka?" That was the name that had come up in her reverse address search.

"There's no one here by that name."

"They live at one-oh-three—"

"That's next door." Dr. Sano pointed to the house to the left. "Goodbye."

Kiku was about to draw her pistol when Daichi appeared behind the doctor and pressed his gun against the back of the man's head.

"Remove the chain and step back, please." Daichi's voice was calm and charming. To Kiku's surprise, Dr. Sano showed no visible sign of distress as he followed Daichi's commands—his hand didn't shake, his breathing was even. Maintaining eye contact with him, Kiku slipped inside the house and shut the door behind her.

Dr. Sano said quietly, "The safe is in the upstairs bedroom."

"You are very calm, Doctor. That is a good thing." In an aside to Daichi, Kiku added, "Clear the house while the doctor and I have a conversation in the kitchen."

Beads of sweat appeared on the doctor's brow—his first sign of nerves. "I'm the only one here. There's another safe in there." He started to point to the room across the hall, but Kiku shook her head.

"Be very careful with those hands, Doctor. Now walk."

As Daichi went to sweep the rooms, Kiku followed the doctor to an immaculate kitchen. It would have been huge in most houses, but actually felt somewhat small for this grand residence. She pointed to a chair, and the doctor sat down.

Aiming the gun at his heart, Kiku said, "You have a sample from Takeo Nakumora. You and I will go to the clinic together and retrieve it. I hate surprises, so you are going to explain to me right now everything we are going to find there."

Dr. Sano folded his hands in his lap. "Very well. I can do that." He took his time speaking, selecting his words with care. Kiku was impressed with his calm demeanor. Normally, people fell apart when they had a gun to their head.

She took her cell phone from her pocket and laid it on the table. "I should mention that since I detest surprises so much, I tend to be very thorough." She scrolled through the pictures of the staff until she reached the man Daichi had spotted leaving in the blue BMW. "My associates picked up Dr. Sugawara. They are asking him the same questions I am asking you. If your answers do not match up, I will put a bullet in your head."

Dr. Sano's leg started to shake and Kiku relaxed a little. She didn't want the doctor to freak out, but she wanted him a *little* nervous. He knew the lab extremely well and gave her careful, detailed descriptions of the building's security procedures. He even sketched a layout of the lab and marked exactly where Takeo's specimen was being held. Kiku was relieved to hear that they had not yet processed it—which meant there was only the one vial to recover, not multiple samples in different labs.

"The last room is the most secure," the doctor said, "though that's mostly for effect, during tours. It has both a badge reader and a hand scanner."

Kiku swore silently. The doctor and Daichi had a very similar build, and she'd hoped that Daichi could pass as the doctor with just his badge, but now that plan was no longer viable. Since the building had separate security staff for daytime and nighttime shifts, and Dr. Sano said he was rarely in the office after hours, the evening shift wouldn't recognize him. The doctor would have to be present in order to gain access to that last room.

"Do you personally take people on tours of the facility?" Kiku asked.

The doctor shook his head. "I don't interact with clients at all."

"What about other doctors? Do they take people on tours?"

Dr. Sano nodded. "Some do."

Daichi returned from having searched the house and walked into the kitchen. His skin was gray and he looked sick. His eyes were the blackest Kiku had ever seen them, completely impenetrable, and his haunted stare was focused on the doctor.

"Why?" Daichi asked.

Dr. Sano sat up straighter as he faced Daichi. His mouth twisted up into a smug little grin. "Everyone needs a hobby. They were my little test subjects."

Daichi drew his gun and shot the doctor between the eyes.

4

Kiku stood in disbelief as the doctor's body fell to the tile floor.

"What is *wrong* with you?" Her voice dropped so low it came out in a growl. Daichi's gun had a silencer, but there was still a risk that a neighbor might have heard the gunshot. And more importantly ... "We needed him alive," she fumed.

Daichi stared down at the body with a look of pure hatred. Then, without a word, he turned and walked out of the kitchen. Kiku followed him upstairs. He didn't look or even glance back as he led her to a door at the end of the hall.

She eyed Daichi curiously. He stood with his back to her, but answered her unasked question as if he had psychic powers. "I smelled death," he whispered.

Kiku smelled it, too.

She kept her gun out in front of her as she approached the tiny room lit by a bare bulb hanging from the ceiling. It contained only three things: a mat, a doll, and a malnourished dead girl chained to the wall. She didn't look like she'd been dead very long.

Kiku was turning away when she noted faint scratches on the floor and finally made out a single word: Rirī. *Lilly*.

That was Daichi's wife's name. Maybe the coincidence had pushed him over the edge. Or maybe it was just that deep down, Daichi was a good man. Either way, she now understood why he'd killed the doctor.

Still, without Dr. Sano ...

Kiku grabbed Daichi by the arm. "You need to come downstairs."

Daichi shook his head.

"The police will find her. They will give her a proper burial."

This time Daichi let her guide him down the hall. But when they reached the kitchen, he lifted his gun and shot the doctor in the head again.

"He is already dead," Kiku said.

"He said, '*They* were tests.' Lilly wasn't the only one. If I could bring him back, I would, just so I could kill him over and over." Daichi's eyes narrowed, and he looked at Kiku. "What did you mean when you said we needed him alive?"

Kiku pointed at the blood-splattered sketch on the table. "The room with the sample is locked. You need a hand scan to open it."

Daichi swore. "Oops."

"This is a little worse than *oops*." Kiku started opening kitchen drawers.

Daichi couldn't seem to take his gaze from the dead doctor. "When this guy doesn't show at work tomorrow and they can't reach him, they'll increase security. We have to get in there tonight. Can your friend find someone else?"

"I have a plan. Hold on." Kiku found superglue and tape and set them on the counter. She then pulled several knives from the butcher block.

Daichi's eyebrows rose. "Are you making something?"

"You could say that. You need to go upstairs and put on some of the doctor's clothes." Kiku's expression softened. "Do not go in that room. The girl's spirit is gone. That is just a husk up there now." She opened a cabinet and pulled out a plastic trash bag. "Also, you ruined the doctor's glasses, so look for another pair."

Daichi shook his head. "I don't look enough like the doctor to pass close inspection."

Kiku cut three holes in the trash bag and draped it over her head like a poncho. "Then you will not let anyone get close enough to inspect. It will be night security anyway, and Dr. Sano did not work nights. Scowl and they will keep their distance."

"You're forgetting one important thing." Daichi held up his good hand and waved it back and forth. "I can't get by the hand scanner. We have to find some other employee. We need to get going."

"There is no time to get another employee. You are going to be the doctor."

"What about the hand scanner?"

Kiku laid the doctor's arm flat on the floor and picked up a knife. "I can give you a hand with that."

5

Daichi parked Dr. Sano's Lexus in the space reserved for him at the fertility clinic. He wouldn't have thought that having a dead man's hand taped and glued onto his own arm would bother him so much, considering the time it had taken to get used to his prosthetic hand. But of all the vile things he had done in his life, this gruesome act was going to haunt him for some time.

His nightmares were quite crowded now. He usually shuffled through a dozen of them at any one time. Like some mental movie theater, his mind would play those dreams for a week or two—and then a new reel of nightmares would replace them. Tonight was guaranteed to be a blockbuster.

Seeing Takeo lying in a coffin, his skin gray, was certain to join the show, too. So was smothering Kiku and sliding her into the morgue refrigerator. Those would join the classics: killing his own father and finding Itsumi floating face up in the pool. At first he had thought she was waiting for him, floating on her back, staring up at the stars ...

Daichi tried to press the metal hook of his prosthetic against his thigh, a trick he'd developed to break out of his waking dreams of hell. But this time, it didn't work because he didn't feel metal jam into his leg but something squishy—

And instead of being even more disturbed by this, Daichi burst out laughing. If he wasn't already crazy, he had a feeling he would be by the time they left Japan.

He got out of the car and strode toward the entrance, scanning the massive lobby through the glass front wall. There was only one guard there, sitting behind a desk and looking at a computer, but he had seen another making rounds earlier. At the front door, Daichi swiped Dr. Sano's card through the scanner. The light turned green. He held his cell phone to his ear as he opened the door.

The guard at the desk stood up suddenly, slamming his laptop closed. His face reddened and he pulled down the hem of his jacket and straightened his belt.

Daichi swore under his breath. Now that the guard was worried his extracurricular activity had nearly been discovered, he would be sure to try to overplay his guard duties and check Daichi's credentials.

Daichi pretended to be talking on his phone as he strode straight toward the elevator. "What is it now?" he snapped. "I'm back at the office. That new girl screwed up again."

The guard came around his desk and moved to cut Daichi off.

Daichi didn't slow his pace. "No, no, I'm not putting up with it." He held the phone between his shoulder and ear as he flashed his badge at the guard. "I'm going to HR in the morning and making certain she's fired. Yes, fired. I certainly didn't become the head of fertility to have my opinions questioned by an assistant."

The guard stopped and folded his hands in front of himself. He let Daichi pass.

"It's too late. She screwed up the labeling process again, too. I'll have to do it myself." Daichi pressed the button for the third floor, but he kept the phone pinned between shoulder and ear, pretending to listen.

The elevator door opened and he stepped in, still keeping the phone to his ear. In all probability the guard had gone back to his porn, or whatever he was doing, but on the off chance he would check the elevator's camera feed, Daichi had to maintain the show. He fired off a few choice swear words before jamming the phone back into his pocket.

The elevator door dinged and Daichi stepped out. The other guard was at the end of the hall, coming this way. He bowed his head at Daichi. Daichi returned the gesture and headed in the opposite direction. He could hear the guard's footsteps behind him—following. Because he suspected something? Or was this just his usual route?

Daichi walked down the hallway with purpose, grateful his long legs would make his quick pace seem natural. But when he rounded a corner, he hesitated. Dr. Sano's sketch of the building was burned into Daichi's memory. Recalling things like that had always come easily to him, even as a child. But that sketch didn't match what Daichi was seeing. The hallway ahead, which should have stretched out a long way in front of him, ended after only twenty feet.

A doorknob behind him rattled, soon followed by another. The guard was probably checking if an office was locked. Daichi's thoughts went in two directions. One side of his brain was trying to work out another route; the other pondered a disturbing thought: had Dr. Sano lied about the building's layout? And if he'd lied about that, he could have lied about the sample, too.

Daichi took out his cell phone and pulled up the picture he'd taken of Dr. Sano's sketch. When he zoomed in, he breathed a sigh of relief. The doctor hadn't lied, and the sketch wasn't incorrect. Daichi had only assumed the hallway continued straight because of a rather large blood spot covering the middle of the map. Instead, he merely had to take a couple of turns to get around the blood spot ... and back on track.

He followed the new route to the specimen room, and the guard's footsteps continued behind him. Daichi quickly swiped his card. The light turned green and the hand scanner lit up. Daichi awkwardly lifted the dead hand and placed it on the scanner. Beneath the hand a green light shone—and then turned red.

Daichi examined the dead hand. Apart from its grayish color, it looked to be in good shape. Perhaps a little puckered. And ... dry?

Swearing under his breath, he wet his lips and licked each finger and the thumb. Trying not to vomit, he swiped his card again, then placed the damp dead hand on the scanner just as the guard turned the corner.

The green scanning light came on again. Daichi held his breath. The scanner turned a solid green. Daichi pulled the door open and slipped inside. So far, so good—but he was waiting for a special sound, and when he didn't hear it, the hairs on the back of his neck stood up.

He glanced over his shoulder. The door hadn't closed and the guard stood in the doorway with a gun pointed at Daichi's chest.

"Don't make any sudden moves." The guard spoke in Japanese, but there was something off about his accent.

Daichi shook his head. "You've got to be kidding me."

"Raise your hands." The guard stepped into the room, the door clicking closed behind him.

Daichi raised his arms, trying to keep the dead hand from flopping back.

"I need the sample of Takeo Nakumora, Dr. Sano," the guard said. "Give it to me and I leave. Simple as that."

The pieces clicked together. Kenzo would have no reason to steal the sample because he already had unfettered access. And now Daichi placed the guard's accent: Russian. Cade Novikov must have found out why Kenzo was in Sendai, and he, too, wanted to steal the sample.

But Daichi had something besides a dead man's hand up his sleeve: this guy believed Daichi was Dr. Sano.

"Don't make me ask twice, Doctor," the fake guard said.

Daichi started to shake and tried to work up some tears, but he'd never been good at crying on demand. "Please ... don't hurt me. I'll get it for you."

He walked over to a cabinet of refrigerated drawers, eerily similar to the morgue refrigerators. The drawers were labeled with numerical codes. Dr. Sano's information had all been good up until now. The man followed, keeping a four-foot distance. Daichi noted the drawer labeled with the code Sano had given him and then opened a different drawer. Icy air rushed up at him when he lifted the metal lid, and his breath made a cloud of condensation as he said, "The sample is very fragile. You must make sure you don't—"

He flung the thermos at the man's face and kicked him backward into an ornate glass wall imprinted with the company logo. The glass shattered. Before the Russian could gather his wits, Daichi kicked his wrist, sending the gun skidding along the glass-covered floor and out of reach.

The Russian leapt to his feet with the skill of a trained martial artist, immediately took up a fighting stance, and then kicked with a sweeping roundhouse. Daichi was not taken completely by surprise—he blocked the kick—but the blow still sent him staggering into a cabinet, and the Russian then punched Daichi in the face twice.

Daichi bear-rushed the smaller man, picked him up off the floor, and drove forward until he smashed him into the far wall. But Novikov's guard was well trained and blunted the impact by bracing his feet against the wall as he hit. Then he raised both arms over his head and brought them down on Daichi's head.

Still holding the Russian, Daichi crashed down on his back, feeling bits of broken glass jabbing him. The other man was twenty years younger and pinned him with the skill of an Olympic wrestler, then rained punches down on him. Only Daichi's right arm was free, and it was useless. He tried hitting the man with his stump, but with the counterfeit hand flopping at the end, it was like slapping the man with a dead fish.

He had been in enough fights to know it would be over soon if he didn't do something fast. He summoned the part of himself that caused him the most shame, had gotten him in the most trouble, and had also saved his life more than once: the vicious anger that simmered beneath the surface. No matter how he tried to change, no matter how much Lilly prayed for him, that raw hatred was always lurking, dormant but ready to open its eyes and roar to life.

A left hook knocked his head into the tile, and Daichi found himself staring at the glass shards beside him.

Yes.

He gave his adversary a bloody grin. With a quick movement, he slammed the dead man's palm down onto the shards of glass so they were embedded in the flesh. Then he slapped the Russian across the face with the macabre weapon. The man screamed, both hands going to his face. That was all the opening Daichi needed. He drew his gun and killed the Russian with two quick shots. Panting, he rolled the body off him and struggled to his feet.

His chest hurt—probably some cracked ribs. His lip was bleeding and the side of his face was already swelling. But he was okay. He fumbled for his phone. He needed to warn Kiku that the Russians were here. But the phone's screen was cracked and it wouldn't power on.

Swearing, he retrieved the Russian's gun and then carefully removed Takeo's sample from its refrigerated drawer. He stuck the gun in his pocket and the thermos in his waistband. As he was preparing to leave, something occurred to him. If the man posing as a guard was a Russian, the guy in the lobby might be, too. And there would be no sneaking up on that guy, not with the video cameras in the hallways and elevator.

He removed the dead man's shirt and hat and put them on. His ruse would buy him at most a second or two—especially now that the shirt was soaked in blood—but that could make all the difference in a gunfight.

Keeping his head down, he staggered back to the elevator. He got in and slumped against the side. Hiding his gun in front of himself, he pressed the button for the ground floor.

A moment later, the elevator dinged, the door opened, and Daichi stepped out. The guard at the front desk turned around, his gun raised. It wasn't the same guard as before—this guy was bigger. And judging by the tightness of his uniform, he had taken it off the original guard.

"Help!" Daichi mumbled in Russian without lifting his head.

The guard lowered his gun, and Daichi killed him with three rapid shots.

Sticking the gun back into his waistband, Daichi scanned the lobby. The Russians were known for sending squads of no fewer than four men—which meant there were at least two more waiting for him. He kept his head down as he strode to the front door and stepped outside.

It wasn't until he heard the short, high whistle that he allowed himself to exhale. That was the all-clear signal. Daichi jogged to the parking lot. Kiku was waiting for him next to a white van. Inside, both the passenger and driver were dead.

"Thanks for coming in for me," Daichi said with a scowl.

"I texted you."

"Phone died"—he held up the thermos—"but I got it."

"How many men inside?" Kiku started walking over to their car.

"Two that I know of." Daichi fell into step beside her. "It has to be Novikov."

Kiku nodded. "The three men in the van were Russian. One was in the back." She didn't look at him as she said, "I am sorry it took me so long to identify them. I was too busy watching the building. I did not even think that someone *else* would be breaking in here, too."

"No reason to apologize." Daichi got into the passenger seat. "Novikov's getting smarter. The two inside were Japanese nationals. I didn't make them until one attacked me."

"Are you hurt?"

"No." Daichi grimaced as he held up the dead hand bristling with glass spikes. "But can you get this off me?"

"As soon as we get back." Kiku started out of the parking lot. "We must get out of here. Once Kenzo is without the seed of his dynasty's future, he will not kill Takeo."

Daichi nodded, but the truth was, he wasn't certain. He knew and feared the beast that lived inside him, but it was nothing compared to the one his brother harbored. Kenzo was evil incarnate, and Daichi knew there was almost nothing that could stop him.

6

Kiku and Daichi sat at the kitchen table while Olivia washed her hands at the sink. It had been three days since they'd stolen Takeo's sample from the clinic, and Kiku had destroyed it—but the damage was done. Takeo lay gravely wounded in the next room. His fever had gone down a little, but he was still unconscious, and the doctor looked concerned.

"Has he spoken?" Kiku asked. Olivia had barred anyone else from entering his room.

Olivia grimaced and gazed back with tired eyes. "Mumblings. Sometimes trauma victims seem stuck in the moment. He keeps muttering *run*."

Kiku sipped her tea. She refused to think of Takeo as a victim. He would overcome this. And she would do whatever was necessary to help him.

"I'm hoping to try a different antibiotic," Olivia said. "I sent Jimmy out for one this morning."

"When did you send him?" Kiku asked.

Daichi responded before Olivia could answer. "You've got to cut him some slack, kid. He hit three clinics in Sendai and the main hospital. He's having to branch out to get stuff, but he's doing everything he can to make up for his screw-up."

Kiku stared into her tea. Maybe Daichi was right. But she'd never had an easy time letting go of anything.

"Have you spoken to Jiro?" she asked.

Daichi shook his head. "No. Neither has Jimmy. All of our calls have gone to voicemail since we hit the fertility clinic. I left a message saying it looked like you were behind it, but at this point … I have to think that Jiro is onto me."

They both stood as they heard a car pull into the driveway.

Daichi looked out the kitchen window. "It's Jimmy."

Kiku noticed his tight expression. "What's wrong?"

"He has a new ride."

A minute later, Jimmy limped in the door. His shirt was torn and his arm was bleeding.

"What happened?" Kiku and Daichi asked in unison.

"A hospital security guard saw me." Jimmy limped over to the sink and poured himself a glass of water. "And not a fake cop either." He drank the entire glass and refilled it.

"Did you get the medicine?" Kiku asked.

Jimmy pulled three bottles from his pocket and tossed them to Kiku.

"Let me see your arm," Olivia said. "What did you cut it on?"

Jimmy shrugged. "Glass or maybe a metal screen. I jumped out a window."

"You need stitches. I'll get my kit." Olivia hurried out of the room.

"Where did you get the car?" Daichi asked.

"I had to lift it. The cops were all over the clinic in a couple of minutes. I didn't want to risk going back." Jimmy finished the glass of water. "I'll move it in a minute."

Kiku headed for the door. "No. I will."

"Wait," Jimmy said. "I got bad news."

Kiku stopped. Daichi crossed his arms and leaned against the counter.

Jimmy looked nervously at Kiku. "Word's hit the street. I haven't verified it, but the guy I heard it from was straight about the clinic. Anyway, he said Kenzo and Novikov have made an alliance."

Daichi chuckled in disbelief. "You mean they've called a truce?"

Jimmy's face lost even more of its color. "No. An *alliance*. They're working together. They want Takeo and Kiku dead. They're offering a huge bounty. Twenty million—ten apiece."

"But Kenzo must realize that we've destroyed Takeo's sample," Kiku said.

"I guess my brother values his own life more than his precious dynasty," Daichi said.

Kiku frowned. "You are taking this news calmly." She sat down again and nodded to Jimmy. "Thank you for getting the medicine. In light of this news, I will not move the car for you. I should lie low." She sipped her tea.

Jimmy nodded. "You're welcome. Look, I'm so, so—"

Daichi smacked Jimmy in the back of the head, cutting him off. "Don't ever bring it up again to her. Ever."

Jimmy nodded to Daichi and then to Kiku.

"Go see Olivia. You're bleeding on the floor," Daichi said.

Jimmy grabbed some paper towels. He pressed some against his arm and used the others to wipe up the blood drops on the floor. "What are we going to do?"

"You're going to get stitched up." Daichi grabbed Jimmy's shirt collar and made him stand. "We'll talk about the rest when you're done."

Jimmy walked into the hallway. "Olivia?"

"Upstairs!" she yelled. "Come on up."

Daichi walked over to the counter, poured himself a cup of tea, and sat down. A grin slowly grew on his face.

"What are you thinking about?" Kiku asked.

"I'm wondering how much Kenzo would offer for me if Jiro told him I was alive."

Kiku's teacup rattled on the saucer as she set it down. "This is not a competition."

Daichi shrugged. "I can't help it. I mean, my brother *really* hates me. I am certain he would offer more for me than for you. I win." He raised his teacup like he was toasting her and took a gulp.

"If Kenzo found out you are alive, he would know that I spared your life and faked your death. Then his hatred for me would know no bounds. He would raise the bounty on me." Kiku held up her teacup proudly. "I win."

Daichi laughed. "I suppose I have to concede defeat. Besides, the others would not contribute much to my bounty. Novikov doesn't even know me. He hates you, though, and so does Jiro."

"Why does Jiro hate me?" Kiku crossed her arms. "I rescued him from his kidnappers and saved his life, for which Kenzo rewarded me handsomely."

"Yeah, about that." Daichi leaned back in his chair. "Do you know why Jiro was at the nightclub when he got kidnapped? He was trying to make a deal with Cade Novikov, and Novikov grabbed him instead."

Kiku bristled. The fool had walked straight into a trap yet failed to learn his lesson. It bothered her beyond measure that she had risked her life to save the traitor. "You still have not explained why Jiro hates me."

"Because his brother relied on you and not on him."

Kiku scowled. She had not failed to notice the way Takeo looked at his nerdy little brother Jiro from time to time, with disdain or disappointment. It had nothing to do with his being sickly or needing glasses and a hearing aid. Takeo was not like that. Kiku was sure it was the weakness of Jiro's soul that bothered Takeo. He couldn't trust Jiro and, in the Yakuza, trust is everything.

"That is no reason to hate *me*," said Kiku.

"Jiro sees you as the reason that he is not Takeo's right hand. Jealousy is a powerful motivator, Kiku. In Jiro's eyes, you have come between two brothers and usurped his brotherly rights—not to mention called into question his manhood, which he has been trying to prove with every short skirt he sees. The green-eyed monster has driven many to kill for less."

Kiku looked away but was unable to hide her grimace. Daichi was right.

"What Jiro fails to see is that he put himself in a lesser position with his own weakness of character and cowardice. Don't fault yourself for being loyal and strong, Ōkami." Daichi stared into the dark waters of his tea as if he were searching for answers. "We need to get you out of Japan, and make sure everyone knows that you have left."

"I cannot leave Takeo."

"Olivia has said Takeo can't be moved. You know that."

"Then we go after Kenzo. Cut the head off the snake."

"No." Daichi set his tea down and leaned his elbows on the table. "We go after Novikov. Everyone will know we left Japan and they'll stop looking here—which makes Takeo safer. If we take out Novikov, the reward drops by half—and we show what will happen to anyone who crosses you."

"You are oversimplifying again. Taking down Novikov is impossible. His home is a fortress."

"Every fortress has a weakness."

"It was one of Stalin's bunkers."

"If Stalin built it, then it has *many* flaws." Daichi laughed.

Kiku's scowl cracked, and she chuckled. "You are playing with our lives."

"We could always run and hide."

Kiku took out her phone. "No. But if we are going after Cade, we need help. I am calling a friend."

7

"Are you both ready to go?" Kiku asked as she walked into the kitchen. "He is on his way."

Daichi and Jimmy nodded.

"Are you certain he can get us out of Japan and to Russia?" Jimmy asked. "There's a lot of heat."

"I am sure."

The door of the room where Takeo was being kept on life support opened, and Kiku couldn't help her heart from jumping at the image of her lover walking out, tall and healed, with a smile on his handsome face just for her. But, as usual, it was Olivia who came out, closed the door behind her, and joined them.

Brushing back a strand of blond hair that had broken free of her bun, she smiled at Kiku. "He's awake now, and his fever has broken. That last antibiotic did the trick." She nodded in gratitude to Jimmy.

Daichi slammed his hand down on Jimmy's back. Kiku was certain he meant it as a compliment, but Jimmy almost fell over.

"Has he said anything?" Kiku asked.

Olivia's eyes met hers. "Yes. He won't stop asking about you."

"Please tell him that I am fine. I will speak with him when I return."

Kiku picked up her bag and strode to the door, ignoring the unasked questions on all their faces. Let them think she was cold-hearted. She knew that leaving this way was the kindest thing she could do for Takeo. And he knew her—knew what he meant to her. Words were unnecessary.

Jimmy followed her hesitantly. They hadn't been alone together since the garage in Sendai just before Takeo was shot. She'd decided to forgive his earlier stupidity, but she hadn't told him that. He still feared her, and she preferred it that way.

Perhaps I got so mad at Jimmy because Jiro duped me, too.

She wondered again why Jimmy had stayed with them. His loyalty had been to Jiro. Had it really shifted to Takeo?

Kiku put her bag in the trunk. "Jimmy? A word."

Jimmy approached with all the enthusiasm of a child going to the principal's office, his hands thrust into his pockets, and stopped a few feet away from her.

"Why are you coming with me?"

Jimmy looked her in the eye and his gaze was steady, if wary. A very good sign; he might be growing up. "I'm on your side, I swear, and—Can I talk about it? Daichi said to never bring it up again, but you just did, right?"

"Three of us are going after Novikov. Odds are we will die. I ask again, why are you coming?"

Jimmy's eyebrows traveled in different directions. "You did say something about getting a lot of money."

"Jiro can give you a lot of money."

Jimmy shook his head firmly. "He betrayed his brother and his father. What would I be to him?"

He'd made a good point, but he still hadn't answered her question.

"Why have you chosen to follow Takeo?" Kiku asked.

Jimmy shrugged. Kiku waited.

"I didn't choose to follow Takeo." Jimmy looked up at her, his brown eyes connecting with hers for a moment before darting away. "I guess I'm choosing you. You could've let me drown in that lake. And you could've died trying to save me. But you came back for me. I'm just a foot soldier, and you're like ..." He trailed off.

"The bad-ass queen!" Daichi called from the back door.

Jimmy looked down, clearly embarrassed.

"Hey! I'm joking!" Daichi called. "I'm just hurt you don't see me the same way."

They all got in the car, with Kiku driving and Daichi providing directions. Fifteen minutes later they were back in the alley where they had switched from the hearse to the flower truck. As soon as they had gotten out and unloaded their bags, an older man appeared at the back door of the restaurant, got behind the wheel, and drove the car away.

Kiku and Jimmy followed Daichi into an office at the back of the restaurant. It was surprisingly spacious, and one wall was loaded with monitors displaying camera feeds from everywhere inside the restaurant.

"You might as well make yourselves comfortable," Daichi said, gesturing toward a couch along the wall.

Jimmy sat down, but Kiku stood and watched the video feeds. A stretch limo pulled up to the entrance. Almost a dozen people got out, and among them she spotted Albert's curly hair and smiling face. Albert Arzamastsev was an art dealer, business acquaintance and dearly devoted friend to Kiku, although Alberts's affections ran much, much deeper. He'd do anything she asked of him.

"That's them?" Daichi asked.

"Yes. We need to wait until the short man with the curly hair asks for the check."

The group came inside and sat down for dinner, chatting away amicably. The three of them watched silently until the diner's entrees came, and Jimmy licked his lips.

He shifted forward on the couch. "Since we're in a restaurant ..."

"No," Kiku said, never taking her eyes off the monitor.

"Watching people eat is making me hungry," Jimmy grumbled.

"I told you to eat something before we left." Daichi swiveled around in the office chair. "What about the steak and rice I made last night?"

Jimmy made a face.

"You never complained before."

"It was the only food in the house. What choice did I have?"

"You seriously don't like my cooking?"

"Will you two stop it?" Kiku snapped. "You sound like an old married couple."

Both men crossed their arms and scowled at each other.

After another twenty minutes of awkward silence, Jimmy muttered, "Sorry."

"It's all right." Daichi was flipping through a magazine on the desk and didn't look up.

"I like your cooking fine. I had a bowl for lunch. It's just, watching them eat lobster is killing me."

Daichi closed the magazine. "If you're that hungry I can see if the kitchen can make you something."

"No time," Kiku said. "Albert asked for the check. That's our signal. You two go to the men's room." She headed for the door. "Take off all your clothes and wait for your men."

"That is not happening," Daichi said, crossing his arms. "I'll change clothes when they arrive. I'm not standing around in the bathroom in my underwear."

Jimmy nodded his agreement.

"I do not have time to argue with your foolish male pride," Kiku said. "Do it now. And do it fast, or I will go into the men's room and shoot you both."

Kiku yanked the door open and walked calmly to the ladies' room. She entered the accessible stall, stripped down to her underwear, and waited.

She did not wait long before a woman pushed the stall door open and slipped inside. Even Kiku thought that this woman's resemblance to her was eerie. Albert had done a fantastic job of finding a double for her, and she was confident he'd done as well for Daichi and Jimmy.

Within two minutes she and her body double had swapped personas, and Kiku left the bathroom. Jimmy was waiting for her in the hallway, dressed in a dark suit.

"Where is Daichi?" Kiku asked.

"Combing his hair," Jimmy said apologetically.

"Get him."

Just then Daichi strolled out of the men's room looking like he owned the place, and it dawned on Kiku that he probably did. Daichi had owned a hundred properties and investments all over Japan before being declared dead, and since they were all acquired under various aliases, he still owned them even after his "death." Now, wearing a dark-gray Armani suit and wire-rimmed glasses, he appeared to be in his element.

They walked to the table where Albert's entourage was seated, and together they all exited the restaurant and entered the waiting limo, the group still chatting away like nothing was amiss. Kiku was surprised at how well Albert played his part. Their eyes met a few times, and he looked like he was bursting to ask her all the questions he had, but he didn't say a word.

The drive to the airport was quick, but as they waited for security to check their paperwork, time slowed to a crawl. Kiku knew Albert's forgers were the best in the world and their passports were flawless, but any number of the security guards at Sendai airport could be working for Kenzo—which meant they would be searching for her. But the security check, though thorough, went smoothly, and soon they were all filing out to the tarmac and to Albert's jet.

As Daichi settled into the seat next to Kiku, he leaned over and whispered, "You have powerful friends."

Kiku nodded. Only time would tell if they were powerful enough to help her bring down Cade Novikov.

8

When they were in the air, Albert sat down in a swivel chair, gesturing to Kiku to take the seat next to him. Daichi motioned to Jimmy and they both moved to the rear of the plane.

"I am afraid I am amassing a debt I will never be able to repay," said Kiku.

Albert held her hand and raised an eyebrow. "These are gifts. You owe me nothing. I only ask that you consider my lopsided offer."

Kiku sighed. Albert had proposed to her twice—elaborately—before she begged him to stop. He had acquiesced, but he didn't refrain from occasionally reminding her that his offer was still on the table.

He patted her hand. "Just think about it. That's all."

Kiku nodded. She knew her answer would not change. But she would do as he requested and consider his offer again—if she survived to do so.

"I got the schematics that you requested," Albert said. "Would you like me to have a table set up for viewing them?"

Kiku squeezed his hand. "Thank you. For everything."

Soon a table was set up, and the four of them took up seats around the blueprints of Novikov's compound. His mansion in Samara—a good-size city straddling two rivers, the Volga and the Samara—sat atop an enormous hill with a spectacular view of the bustling city and gorgeous river valley below. A bunker had been discovered there, built in 1942 as an exact replica of Stalin's Moscow bunker, complete with an underground tunnel system. There was only one road in, and no other homes or buildings for miles. Novikov had the money and power to make sure he had no neighbors.

"We cannot use the road; he will see us from a mile off," Kiku said. "And the only way to come from the other side is up the mountain, and most of it is bare rock. I can make it, but ..." She glanced meaningfully at Daichi's prosthetic.

"I can climb with one arm," Daichi said confidently.

Kiku had her doubts, but she wouldn't call him out in front of the others.

"I'll try it," Jimmy offered.

Daichi shook his head. "A night climb is not the best time to learn."

Kiku tapped the blueprints in frustration. "We have the entire layout of the mansion, but we cannot get close enough to do anything."

"Albert," Daichi said, "how did you get your hands on these blueprints?"

"*War-torn Masters* just did a special on Stalin's inner circle."

"That's the other TV show Albert's on," Jimmy whispered. "*Big Boy Toys* is the one I watch."

Daichi nodded. "I'm not really a big TV watcher. Sorry."

"No apologies necessary." Albert smiled. "I'm just a guest on the shows anyway. A sort of independent expert."

"Novikov let his house be featured on the show?" Kiku asked.

"No—one of the producers told me that Novikov closed off that possibility pretty quickly. But they got the layout of all of Stalin's properties from the archives. After Stalin's Great Purge, he had the mansions set up as fortresses for the six generals who formed his inner circle."

"And what expertise did you provide for this show?" Daichi asked.

"Stalin also provided those generals with priceless artworks that the Nazis had stolen. *War-torn Masters* brought in ground-penetrating radar to see if they could find any pieces still hidden. I was supposed to authenticate whatever they found, but unfortunately the episode that I'm featured in was a bust. It was centered around General Romanov's summer fortress, and they found nothing there."

"Can we use the show somehow?" Jimmy asked. "Could that be our way in?"

Kiku nodded thoughtfully. "We could pose as producers. That would get us through the gates. A Trojan horse."

Daichi frowned. "It will take too long. Novikov's on the warpath. He might not expect us to come to him, but he'll be ready."

"Ideally, we lure him out," Kiku said. "You or I can then take a sniper shot. Otherwise, he heads to the safe room and he's out of our reach. At that point we could blow up the entire mountain and he'd be untouched." She noticed Albert shaking his head. "What is it, Albert?"

Albert hesitated. "I'm the last person to tell you how to handle your affairs ... but the safe room is where he's most vulnerable."

"I think you're right, Albert," Jimmy said with a slight eye roll. "You should leave planning to them."

Kiku glared at Jimmy, then said to Albert, "Please explain."

Albert took a deep breath. "When *War-torn Masters* used the radar to search for hidden rooms at Romanov's summer fortress, they found a small shaft that led down to several intersecting load-bearing beams."

Kiku, Daichi, and Jimmy exchanged puzzled glances.

Albert closed his eyes and clicked his fingers. "It's like the American movie. The one with the little green alien." He opened one eye and gazed at them hopefully.

"*E.T.*?" Daichi asked.

"He is not green," Kiku said.

"Yoda?" Jimmy said, his eyes lighting up. "*Star Wars*!"

"Yes." Albert nodded. "But the movie before Yoda. The first one."

"*A New Hope*?" Jimmy asked. "The one with the Death Star?"

"Yes!" Albert said excitedly. "My point is that Stalin didn't trust anyone—not even his inner circle. So, in the event of another rebellion, he had a plan. If the generals betrayed him and fled to the safe room, he could slip in a small explosive and bring the whole house down on top of them."

"But that was a different house," Daichi pointed out.

"It was the same architect. And Stalin commissioned them all."

Kiku grabbed Albert's head and kissed his cheek.

Daichi clapped him on the back. "You're a freaking genius!"

"Wait! Wait!" Jimmy said. "Did they mention this on the show? If they did, then Novikov has to know about it."

Albert shook his head. "No. The producers are still hoping to gain access to the other mansions and ... well, it's still not smart to say anything bad about Stalin in Russia."

Daichi grinned. "Then he doesn't know. All we have to do is drive the snake into his hole, and then bring it down on his head."

"That still is not an easy feat," Kiku said. "There are only three of us."

"We got this," said Daichi. "Novikov has thirty men, tops." He tapped the blueprint. "I'll take the left flank. Kiku, you take the right. Jimmy ... you're gonna be ... recon."

"Oh, hell no." Jimmy shook his head. "I'm not sitting this out."

Kiku crossed her arms. "Daichi's right. I do not mean to insult you, but it would be suicide for you to go in with us."

"I could wear a bulletproof vest," Jimmy offered.

Daichi chuckled. "You'd need to wear a bulletproof *suit*."

Albert cleared his throat. "I can get you body armor. And I also have the Mighty Ferret."

Jimmy's eyes lit up like a child on Christmas morning. "You have the Mighty Ferret! It was on season three of *Big Boy Toys*!"

Albert smiled. "You *are* a fan."

"What is a Mighty Ferret?" Daichi asked.

"A one-man assault tank!" Jimmy said excitedly. "It's got a top-mounted, belt-fed machine-gun turret. The one on the show was developed for police use and didn't have the machine gun, though." He turned to Albert. "Please tell me the one you have *does* have a machine gun?"

Albert laughed and nodded. Jimmy pumped his fists in the air as if he'd scored a touchdown.

"Would Novikov have the firepower to take down a tank?" Daichi asked.

"I would expect that he would have RPGs," Kiku said. "Can this tank survive that?"

"Yes ..." Albert made a face. "But can the person inside survive it? That's up for debate."

Jimmy's smile dimmed, but only slightly. "The Mighty Ferret will come through. I can bust right in the front door and send Novikov running straight to his safe room. I mean, come on, it's a freaking *tank*!"

Kiku raised an eyebrow at Daichi. He thought for a moment, then nodded.

"How soon could we get this Mighty Ferret there?" Kiku asked.

"I can call now and have them get it ready. It's in my showroom."

Kiku grabbed Albert by the elbow and walked with him to the front of the plane. Behind her, she heard Jimmy giving Daichi the specs of the Mighty Ferret with fanboy excitement.

"Listen, Albert," Kiku said in a low voice. "I appreciate everything, but if we use that tank, Novikov is going to figure out who helped us."

"You will deal with Novikov, so I will not need to worry about ramifications."

Kiku stared deep into his brown eyes. "If this mission fails, Novikov will take everything from you."

Albert reached up hesitantly and brushed Kiku's cheek with his thumb. "If the mission fails, he will have already taken from me everything that matters."

9

Kiku stood at the base of the cliff, gazing up at the black rock and the stars peeking out above. Attached to her back were ten pounds of climbing equipment, another twenty-five pounds of tactical gear, and a twenty-pound cylinder bomb. She didn't like the idea of strapping a bomb to her back, but if it went off, she wouldn't have to worry about it anymore.

Daichi was carrying the same gear, along with a grin from ear to ear. It was at times like these, when death was imminent, that he seemed to be at his best. Kiku was well aware everyone eventually loses to the Angel of Death, but Daichi looked forward to the fight every time.

"Ready?" he asked, eager to go.

Kiku gave a thumbs-up and started to climb. There was no need for words. They had gone over the plan many times and they both knew it by heart. When they reached the top of the ridge, they would split up, Kiku taking the left flank, and rappel down the other side. Then they would wait for Jimmy's signal.

Daichi had swapped his prosthetic hand for a climbing axe attached to his forearm. So far he was keeping up with her, but she worried about whether or not he could maintain her pace. They couldn't afford the luxury of a slow climb.

Kiku reached up to a ledge above her. It was wide enough that she and Daichi could catch their breath there before making their final push. But just as her right arm landed on top of the ledge, the rock beneath her feet broke free, leaving her suspended over the darkness, swinging like a pendulum. She frantically clawed into the gravel with her right hand as she sought a handhold with her left. Most of her weight was on her right forearm, and with each swing, the weight of the equipment dragged her closer to the edge.

She'd made one foolish mistake—letting her guard down before she was safely on the ledge—and now it would cost her her life.

"What's taking you so long?" Daichi grumbled as he grabbed hold of her backpack and lifted her up and onto the ledge.

"Thank you," Kiku panted as she turned around and moved close to the wall, slumping to a sitting position. She silently kicked herself for not arranging for an iron infusion after giving so much blood to Takeo. Anemia meant less oxygen in her blood, and with higher elevations, it could spell disaster.

"I helped you for purely selfish reasons." Daichi stretched. "I didn't feel like taking on fifty guys by myself."

"Ha-ha." Kiku gulped down some water and tried to get her breathing back to normal. "Do you not need a break?"

"A break? I feel like I'm in first gear." Daichi squatted beside her. "I don't mean for this to sound insulting, but I could climb up ahead of you and lower a rope."

Kiku's eyes narrowed and she scrambled to her feet. "I was going slow for *you*, old man."

"That's a good one." Daichi laughed. "And you also slipped to make me feel better about myself? How about you put your money where your mouth is, little girl, and we let the mountain decide. A thousand dollars I beat you to the top."

"Perhaps I was wrong about your age. If you want to step up to the adult betting table, the ante starts at twenty-five thousand."

"Fine. I want to buy Lilly something nice for Christmas. But let's not stop when we reach the top. I will beat you up and then down the other side, too. Set your watch."

"Ready." Kiku opened her stopwatch. "On three, two, one, *go*!" She pressed the button and jumped for the cliff face.

The truth was, her brush with the Angel of Death had rattled her. Maybe Daichi had picked up on that, and that was why he was goading her, but it was exactly what she needed. Kiku's competitiveness drove her fears back into the darkness where they belonged.

On the easy stretches of rock, Kiku flew ahead of Daichi, but on the sections that were more difficult to traverse, his strength and experience gave him the edge. In the end, he reached the top before her—though only by seconds.

They gave each other a thumbs-up, then separated and rushed in opposite directions.

On the other side of the ridge, several lights illuminated the mansion below. Kiku pulled up the schematic from memory and mentally plotted the course she'd take. She'd clear the second floor, get to the stairway in the middle, then sweep back across the first floor. After that, she and Daichi would drive Novikov and his men into the safe room.

And then one of them had to make it to the airshaft to drop the explosive.

Three against fifty. And who knows if this airshaft idea will even work. Luke Skywalker had better odds. And he had the Force.

Kiku anchored her trad gear to the rock, used a carabiner to clip her rope to it, then tossed the coil of rope off the side and into the darkness. As she stepped out into the abyss, her heart beat wildly. But it wasn't due to the usual adrenaline-fueled exhilaration, but rather something far less familiar—fear. In that moment, Kiku didn't know which was more unnerving: the fear of dying, or what was driving it.

Because for the first time in Kiku's adult life, she really wanted to live.

10

When Kiku's feet touched the ground, the sky was already starting to lighten. The sun would soon crest the jagged mountains. She hurried to the shadows of some pine trees, removed her climbing gear, and strapped on her tactical equipment, including a helmet and bulletproof vest. She was armed with three flashbangs, three smoke grenades, and an M4 assault rifle with thirty-round magazines and a side-mounted red-dot sight calibrated to ten feet for closeup work. She also had her SIG-Sauer pistol with five magazines and, of course, the twenty-pound cylindrical bomb.

When she was within sight of the house, she activated the microphone on her tactical helmet. "This is Ōkami," she whispered. "Come in, Onryō."

"I won," Daichi boasted.

Kiku had almost forgotten the contest. "How do you know?"

"My time was ninety-three minutes and twenty-seven seconds."

Kiku grinned. She'd beaten him by a full two minutes. But for the sake of his male pride, she would pretend otherwise. "Fifty grand," she muttered, and swore.

Daichi laughed. "Don't go getting yourself shot, Santa. I need to get Lilly that really nice Christmas present this year, and you're buying."

The headlights of Jimmy's old moving truck, with the Mighty Ferret concealed in the back, appeared in the distance, lumbering up the winding mountain road.

"This is Rudolph. I'm on my way," Jimmy said. "Hey," he added, "can I switch my name to something cooler, like Iron Man?"

Kiku chuckled and Daichi laughed.

"Oh, come on," Jimmy grumbled. "You're the one who picked the stupid name for me."

"Rudolph fits. You're leading the way," Daichi said.

Kiku knew that Daichi had selected the name for a different reason. He'd told her that when Novikov's men saw Jimmy's tank, the metal on the front would glow red from all the bullets hitting it.

Kiku scanned the house for movement. "Are you in place?"

"I'm good. Rudolph ready."

"Ōkami moving."

"Onryō watching." All the mirth had left Daichi's voice, and at the moment he was living up to the name of Onryō—a vengeful spirit who returns to earth to right a wrong. The Daichi of old was back.

Even Kiku didn't know the full story of Daichi's past. All she knew was that he was Kenzo's half-brother, born of a Japanese father and a Chinese mother. In his teens, Daichi showed up in Japan insisting that his father, Kadiri, the head of the Yakuza, recognize him as his son. Kadiri refused and sent two men to throw Daichi back out on the street. Daichi killed them both with a hammer. So Kadiri ordered six more trained killers to try their hand, and this time Kadiri watched, with Kenzo at his side, while Daichi killed all six.

He was only fourteen.

After that, Kadiri often told the tale of the boy who fought like a demon. But Kiku had never believed that the handsome man who reminded her of a movie star could be anything other than kind and gracious, until she saw Daichi in action. It was as if something else, something dark, took over. He became a cold, methodical, heartless specter that brought death to all who stood against him.

After the loss of her sister, an avenging spirit was exactly what Kiku aspired to be. She and Daichi were kindred spirits. And tonight, they would bring death to this house.

Kiku crept down the slope to the corner of the mansion. Its thick stone walls provided plenty of handholds and footholds, making for an easy climb to the second floor. She started her ascent.

A light snapped on at the front of the house. Kiku kept climbing. She reached a second-floor window and peeked inside the small room. A man lay sprawled across the bed in his underwear. She pulled out her pistol as she slid the window open.

The man raised his head and looked down the barrel of her gun.

She pulled the trigger, then swung herself into the bedroom and waited below the window. She set her M4 for three-round bursts, and flipped the gun on its side to use the red-dot sight at such close quarters.

The second the dark-oak bedroom door swung open, she squeezed the trigger. The Russian who'd opened the door fell back into the hallway, his unfired shotgun along with him.

The bedroom door was at the end of a long hallway, giving Kiku a clear shot straight down the corridor. She rotated the M4 again to switch back to the regular sight.

Two men rushed into the hall. She waited until they were both looking at the dead man on the floor before she pulled the trigger again.

Four down. No way to know how many remained. She tossed a smoke grenade and a flashbang into the hallway to disorient anyone nearby, then slipped back out the window and closed it behind her. She climbed sideways along the stone facade, creeping around the corner toward another second-floor window at the front of the mansion.

Novikov's men would be trying to figure out how to counterattack her in the bedroom. And she'd outflank them. At least, that was the plan.

Gunfire erupted in the distance. Daichi had made his entrance.

She passed three windows before reaching the one she wanted, which led to a small library. She silently opened the unlocked window and slipped inside. Novikov's overconfidence and lax security would be his downfall.

The plush Oriental carpet muffled her footsteps as she crossed the floor to peer out into the same hallway she'd just seen from a different angle. Down the hallway, toward the bedroom, four armed men stood on either side of the corridor, facing away from her, trying to peer through the smoke from her grenade. They clearly had no idea that Kiku had outflanked them.

She flipped the M4 onto full auto, aimed, and held down the trigger. As her ammo dwindled, the body count grew. The men's bodies fell to the floor, and her hand was a blur as she jammed in a fresh magazine.

"Ōkami eight."

"Onryō eleven."

Kiku slipped back to the front window and looked out. The old truck had come up to the gates, turned around, and parked.

For a moment, all was still. Then the moving truck's rear doors burst open and the Mighty Ferret came blasting out.

It looked more like a double-decker snowmobile than it did an armored tank. Small enough to fit through a doorway, it had an arrow-head nose, tank treads, and a top-mounted machine gun. It punched through the tall, gated entrance without even slowing.

But Kiku's hopes of Novikov running straight for the safe room were dashed when a storm of lead rained down from the mansion and hundreds of bullets pounded the little tank. Daichi's estimate of thirty men might have been a gross underestimate.

But he'd been correct about one thing: the metal on the nose of the tank started to glow a bright red as each shot pinged off the surface.

"THIS SUCKS!" Jimmy yelled into his microphone, his voice nearly drowned out by the barrage of bullets hammering his vehicle. The turret continued to fire back, but it was no longer turning.

"Ōkami moving."

Kiku sprinted down the hallway toward the center staircase that led down to the front door. Pressing her back against the wall, she peered around the corner. A dozen men stood at the top of the stairs, firing out at the tank through the shattered windows of the two-story front foyer. From the sound of it, there were many more just below them.

"Ōkami tossing bang at stairs."

She tossed a flashbang and opened fire. She took down four men before the others started shooting at her. The corner of the wall next to her disintegrated as gunfire raked its surface. She backed up five long steps and was preparing to circle around when the gunfire suddenly stopped.

"Onryō clear." Daichi's voice was calm.

Kiku peeked around the corner. Daichi had dropped the remaining eight men and was reloading. He tossed a flashbang over the railing into the foyer, followed by a smoke grenade, then stepped right up to the railing and opened fire on the first floor.

Bullets flew upward at him, punching holes in the ceiling, but his expression betrayed not an ounce of concern. He was focused, firing in three-round bursts, as screams erupted below.

Kiku dropped another flashbang over the railing and swung wide, firing as she went.

"Back! Fall back!" someone bellowed in Russian.

The Mighty Ferret's treads pulled it up the marble front steps, and it crashed through the door, machine gun still firing. The Russians turned and bolted.

Daichi slammed a fresh magazine into his gun and started down the stairs with Kiku following. As they had hoped, the Russians had fled down another set of stairs into the cellar. The safe room was guarded by two large metal doors, which were now slammed shut. But the doors had openings in them for gun barrels, and bullets blasted forth. Daichi dove for cover, while Jimmy returned fire.

"You're up, Ōkami!" Daichi yelled into his mic.

Kiku raced down the main hallway to the kitchen. She swept the room with her gun and made certain it was clear before unslinging the explosive canister from her back and setting it down carefully. Then she opened the door to the utility room.

Pain exploded up her back. A bullet had slammed into her bulletproof vest, just above her left kidney. The next shot hit the doorframe next to her head, sending splinters flying.

Kiku fired blindly behind her as she scrambled behind the kitchen island and crumpled to the floor. Her breath came in painful gasps. The bullet-resistant Kevlar plate had stopped the bullet, but it still felt like someone had hit her with a baseball bat.

Bullets whizzed over the counter just above her head. She pressed her belly to the floor. There was a three-inch space beneath the island, which was held up by wooden legs—just enough to see thick Russian boots in the doorway of the pantry. She stuck her gun into the space and fired. When the man fell, she put three more rounds into his body.

Gasping for air, she forced herself to her feet, staggered into the utility room, and yanked open the panel that led to the airshaft. What she saw didn't make it any easier to breathe: a shiny new air duct glistened where the airshaft leading down to the safe room had once been. When she grabbed it and jammed it upward, she revealed a new cement pad that sealed off their only hope of killing Novikov.

"Onryō, abort. Abort." Kiku grabbed the explosive canister and started running back toward the front of the house.

Daichi met her halfway down the hall. "What's the issue?"

"They removed the airshaft. It is gone, sealed with cement. We have to abort."

Daichi shook his head. "No. We have to take out Novikov." He turned and ran back toward the foyer.

Kiku raced along next to him. "Not today. The helicopter is on its way. We have to go."

Daichi stopped beside the tank. "Rudolph! Get out!" he ordered.

The tank door on the side of the vehicle opened and Jimmy flopped out, bright red and bathed in sweat. "What's going on?" he yelled. Even though he had worn earplugs, his ears were probably ringing from the lead hailstorm he'd just endured.

Daichi grabbed the canister from Kiku, removed the matching one from his back, and strapped both of them onto the back of the Mighty Ferret.

"What are you doing?" Jimmy shouted.

"You two get going." Daichi's eyes sparkled, and he flashed his trademark grin. "This is going to work. I know it. This tank will fit down those stairs and it's designed to break through all doors. I'm going to drive the Mighty Ferret right into that safe room and detonate the bombs!"

Kiku slapped him across the face. "You are *not* going to throw your life away in some crazy kamikaze mission."

Daichi made a face. "I didn't mean I'm going to be *in* it. I'll get it moving and let it go down the steps and straight into the door."

Kiku pressed her lips together. "That will work."

Daichi rolled his eyes. "Kiku, arm those things. Jimmy, give me a hand."

Jimmy laughed.

Daichi scowled. "Very funny."

"Use this." Jimmy grabbed a shotgun off the floor and handed it to Daichi.

"Are you set, Ōkami?"

Kiku armed both explosives. "One-minute timer is ... go!"

Daichi wedged the throttle of the tank down with the shotgun, then ran alongside the tank, steering it toward the staircase. "Stand back!"

"Close the door!" Kiku shouted. She could see that the tank's gull-wing door would catch the wall if it was open.

As Daichi slammed the door shut, a fresh hail of gunfire erupted from the safe room and up the stairs. Bullets pinged off the tank, ricocheted off the ceiling, and buzzed all around Daichi like hot embers flying up from a campfire.

"Move!" Kiku screamed.

But Daichi was already dancing backward and out of range. Kiku grabbed his left arm, Jimmy grabbed his right, and all three raced for the front door. The sound of the Mighty Ferret bouncing down the stairs was followed by a deafening ring of metal slamming against metal.

At what was left of the front door, Daichi stopped and turned. And Kiku did the same. She felt like a bystander watching a car accident—she couldn't look away. The three of them gazed at the top of the stairs and waited.

A sound like a giant beast sucking in breath filled the air for a fraction of a second, before fire and smoke roared from the staircase. The blast threw Kiku, Jimmy, and Daichi backward down the steps, and they landed hard on the pavement below.

The pain in Kiku's kidney doubled in intensity. She saw stars and tasted blood in her mouth, but she managed to roll onto her knees. Daichi was already on his feet. He absentmindedly reached down for her as he stared at the black smoke billowing from the mansion's windows.

Jimmy rose unsteadily to his feet and swayed like a drunken soldier. "How do we know if it broke through the door?"

A roar like a dozen freight trains racing past made all three cover their ears. Then the entire mansion shuddered, shook, and crumbled inward, as if being sucked into a hole that steadily grew.

"Run!" Daichi shouted.

The three of them raced away from the destruction and toward the helicopter that had cleared the ridge of the mountain and was heading for a field at the far corner of the estate.

Kiku's ears were ringing, but one sound rose above all the others.

Daichi's laughter.

11

The helicopter flew them straight to the airport, where they transferred to one of Albert's private jets. Soon after boarding, they took off, and were in a climbing ascent in minutes.

"One," Kiku admonished Jimmy as he headed straight for the onboard bar. Kiku sat across from Daichi, both window seats. Daichi stared out at the hilly landscape.

"Oh, come on." Jimmy rolled his eyes. "Lighten up a little. We just took out Novikov. Let's celebrate."

"Our work is not yet done. Now we go after Kenzo. He will make Novikov seem like a backyard barbecue."

Jimmy held up a bottle of Scotch. "*You* want something, right, Daichi?"

"Just water." Daichi's features were stern.

Jimmy looked at both of their serious faces, then frowned and walked past the bar to the refrigerator.

"Is there word on Takeo?" Kiku asked.

Daichi's face softened a little and he turned his gaze towards her. "Olivia said he is stable and more coherent now."

"Is he stable enough to be moved?"

Daichi shook his head. "It would be best if we let him recover for at least a few more days."

"I will feel better when he is back in America."

Jimmy handed them water bottles. "I'll feel better when we're *all* back in America." He flopped down in a chair and opened his own. "Though I've never been."

Daichi stared out the window into the sky. "I'll take you riding."

"Motorcycle?"

"Horse." Daichi smiled.

Jimmy cast a glance at Kiku to see if he was being serious.

Kiku nodded. "Daichi's the original Asian cowboy. Have you been able to reach Jiro?"

"No," said Jimmy.

"Me neither," Daichi said. "What did you leave for a message?"

"That I'm scouring Japan looking for Kiku and Takeo."

"Good. I gave him the same story. My men in America tell me that Jiro was in New York, but there's been no sign of him or his security team for three days."

Kiku crossed her legs and tried to settle back onto the ice pack on her back. "Kenzo is a brilliant man. He must know by now that Jiro was behind the melee at the food court meeting. He may have made his move against Jiro."

"I had two men watching Kenzo," Daichi said. "He's gone dark, too."

"If Kenzo's location is not known, can we draw him to us?" Kiku asked.

Daichi shook his head. "Kenzo is going to be on high alert. We took out Novikov. Even if he thinks we're going after Jiro first, he's unlikely to fall for such a ruse."

"What if we use a decoy and feed false intel to Jiro? We could pretend to be moving Takeo."

Daichi tapped his prosthetic against his leg. "To kill Kenzo, we have to use a sledgehammer or a needle. And I don't think, even with your friend Albert's help, we could get a big enough sledgehammer. We need something subtle, under the radar. It isn't the most honorable way, but my brother is not an honorable man."

Albert stepped into the cabin, followed by a stewardess wheeling a tray of sandwiches. His limp was more noticeable today. "I hope you don't mind the interruption," he said. "I thought you might care for a bite."

Daichi and Jimmy nodded and swiveled around in their chairs. Kiku stood up and winced as the ice pack slid off her back.

Albert frowned. "My apologies. I should have had the foresight to bring a doctor onboard."

Kiku laughed and took him by the arm. "You are the most thoughtful man I have ever met."

"Hey!" Daichi mumbled through a mouthful of food. "Climbing a mountain and taking on a hundred guys with machine guns is thoughtful." He swallowed and smiled. "Just in a different way."

"We are up to a hundred men now? Pretty soon you will have taken on the whole Russian army—"

"Don't say it!" Daichi interrupted her. His sandwich flopped over as he pointed at Kiku.

"Single-handedly," she said.

Jimmy laughed until Daichi kicked him under the table.

Albert smiled, but Kiku noticed the worry in his eyes.

"Come." Kiku led Albert to the back of the plane and eased herself into a chair.

Albert knelt down and gently touched her shoulders. "Is everything okay?"

"I need to make sure *you* are okay, Albert. Someone will replace Novikov, and I am worried they will find out you helped us."

Albert squeezed her hand. "Everything will be fine. Yesterday is over, and tomorrow is not here yet, but today is lonely waiting for you."

Kiku blushed at hearing her words repeated back to her.

"You used to tell me that every day."

Kiku closed her eyes. She could still picture Albert lying in the hospital bed, surrounded by machines and wires.

"I did not know if you could hear me."

"But I could. When I woke up, I asked the doctors where the angel who had watched over me had gone, and I repeated those words. *Everything will be fine. Yesterday is over, and tomorrow is not here yet, but today is lonely waiting for you.* I will never forget them, Kiku. You waited for me, brought me back from the brink."

"I almost got you killed once, Albert. I could not bear to see anything happen to you again."

Albert sat back and smiled. "You may not like hearing this, but that night is one of my fondest memories. Not the part about falling off the balcony, though." He laughed.

Takeo had sent Kiku to a state banquet in Finland, of all places. Albert had bumped into her there, and relentlessly followed her around the party afterwards. She talked to him for what seemed like hours before she finally lost him by slipping out onto a balcony. At that moment a rival of Takeo's decided to strike. He got the drop on her, and he would have shot her if it hadn't been for Albert, who had come looking for Kiku. When he saw the man with the gun, he rushed forward and tackled him. The other man was much bigger and heavier, but Albert clung to the gunman like a rodeo cowboy on a bull. They both slammed into the balcony and fell over the edge. From the fourth floor.

The hitman was killed instantly. His body bore most of the impact, as Albert was on top of him when they landed. But Albert was far from unscathed. He shattered both legs and his pelvis, broke seven ribs, perforated a lung, and ended up in a coma for nearly a month.

Kiku opened her eyes, slightly embarrassed that she had gotten lost in the memory.

"I will be fine," Albert said reassuringly. "My best artist has just finished another portrait of Putin. This one has him at the helm of a sailboat. I will politely ask him for a little more protection."

Kiku laughed. *Such a kind man, but he plays a dangerous game.*

Daichi raised his hand and waved her over, so she asked Albert to excuse her for a moment.

Jimmy's face was white and drawn; he looked like he was going to throw up. He passed by Kiku without saying a word and went into the bathroom.

"Is he okay?" Kiku asked. She eyed the food suspiciously.

"It's not the food." Daichi set his phone down. "We need to go to Hong Kong."

Kiku cast a puzzled look back at the bathroom. Jimmy was from Hong Kong. "Why?"

"Kenzo has Jimmy's sister and her husband."

Kiku's knuckles turned white as she gripped the seat back.

Daichi met her steely gaze. "At least we don't have to go looking for Kenzo. He's luring us out."

12

As Kiku drove the cab down a busy Hong Kong street a steady rain made the lights of the city sparkle in the night. Jimmy and Daichi were in the back seat. They were looking for Jimmy's sister, but he had no idea where she was. Their first stop had been her house. Not surprisingly, they found no sign of her or her husband. And there was no one watching the house.

Kenzo was sweating them out.

"I may know someone who can help," Daichi said. "Head to the Cattle Depot."

Kiku and Jimmy both did a double take.

"This person ..." Kiku stopped at a red light and looked over her shoulder at Daichi. "It is not the Rat King, is it?"

"The Rat King knows everything that goes on in Hong Kong," Daichi said.

"He also wants me dead."

"She poisoned him," Jimmy added.

"I *pretended* to poison him," Kiku clarified. "I used almond extract in place of arsenic."

"What? When?"

"When I came looking for Takeo. I needed to locate him quickly."

"We need to find my sister."

"Then I say we stick to my plan." Daichi grinned roguishly. "Let's go have a chat with the Rat King."

13

Jimmy sat in the back of the cab, staring at the bullet hole in the windshield. His foot was bouncing against the floor, and no matter how hard he tried, he just couldn't seem to stop it.

Come on. Keep it together.

Here he was in a cab with Kiku Inazuka and Daichi Nakumora. He'd dreamed about this when he was a teenager, and now it was happening. But in his fantasies, he'd always kept it together. He'd imagined himself being as cool as them, hanging in the back of the car like a boss—not sniffling like a wimp about to cry.

Yet this was no fantasy. His sister was about to die. He was sure of it. He could picture her being tortured. Fumie, his big sister, who had always been there for him. Who had always been a shield between him and his overbearing, abusive parents, fiercely guarding her little brother. Now it was his turn to repay the debt. And here he was close to tears.

And her husband was probably already dead. What use would Doug be to them? He was American. Maybe they would ... no. Doug would open his big mouth and Kenzo would quickly put a bullet in it.

Jimmy dug his fingernails into his leg. He *had* to keep it together. He'd already messed up so much. His biggest mistake had been trusting Jiro.

Now someone was going after his sister. And even though his error had nearly cost Kiku her life and that of the man she loved, she was helping him.

He leaned his head against the back of the seat and closed his eyes. What a moron he'd been. He'd told Jiro everything about himself. Like a guest sitting on Dr. Phil's couch, he'd bared his soul. Jimmy had been an errand boy for the Yakuza for so long—a perpetual hustler and class clown—and he'd thought this was his big break, his chance to ingratiate himself with the son of the main man. To take the nerdy bookworm under his wing and show him the party side of Hong Kong.

But like everything in his life, Jimmy's success was all in his head.

He took out his pistol and checked the magazine. The last time he'd seen the Rat King, he'd fallen apart. That couldn't happen now. Fumie needed him.

Jimmy was done being a moron. He was going to do whatever it took to get his sister back.

14

Kiku parked the cab in an alley near the Cattle Depot and the three of them got out. She picked up a cinder block and smashed it through the windshield.

Daichi and Jimmy exchanged puzzled glances.

"To the police, a cab with a cinder block on the dashboard and a shattered window raises fewer questions than a cab with a bullet hole in the windshield."

Daichi nodded. "Vandalism is a much better way to go." Then he picked up a rock and broke the back windshield as well.

"Now. What is your plan?" Kiku said.

"You're not going to like it." Daichi explained his plan. And he was right: the longer he spoke, the more Kiku didn't like it.

When he finished, Jimmy nodded in agreement. "I think it will work."

Kiku scowled, but she couldn't think of a better alternative. "Fine."

Jimmy took off his belt. "Put your hands behind your back," he said to her. "Please," he added quickly.

She shook her head. "We are doing this for show. Tie my hands loosely in front of me." She laced her fingers together and pushed out with her wrists as Jimmy tightened the belt. This created slack so she could get out later.

Cheung raised his hand. The red lights disappeared.

"I need information," Daichi continued. "Someone has taken Jimmy Lao's sister and her husband. Who took them, and where are they now?"

Cheung tilted his head, and an older man shuffled out from a hiding spot behind a bookcase. He leaned down beside Cheung, and the two men spoke in low voices for a moment. Then the man shuffled away.

"Is this the couple who live in Causeway Bay?" Cheung asked. "Your sister is Fumie, and her husband is an American cab driver, Doug Miller?"

"Yeah," Jimmy said. "That's them."

"None of my men are responsible for their disappearance, but Doug owes me close to a thousand pounds. He likes betting on the horses more than driving his cab."

"If anyone can find out who has them, you can," Daichi said.

"I can look into it." Cheung leaned back as three women brought two place settings over to the table. "Sit. Let's discuss the Jade Plaza." He pointed a finger at Kiku. "Her, I will not break bread with."

"It would be rude for me to dine with you with her watching," Daichi said. "And there's nothing to discuss as far as the Jade Plaza is concerned, except ... well, since you don't have the information I need, I'll have to alter the deal. I'll tell you what. I'll let the Jade go for two million, and you forget about this little disagreement with Kiku and give us safe passage out of Hong Kong."

Red dots appeared on Daichi's chest once more.

Daichi raised an eyebrow. "Okay. One million. That's my final offer."

"One million?"

Daichi nodded.

"Deal." Cheung folded his hands together and gave a slight bow.

"I'll have my lawyers send you the papers."

"If I am able to locate Fumie and her husband, you will of course forgo the million?" Cheung asked.

"Not a chance," Daichi said. "You need it to look legit anyway. But if you find out any information on Fumie, I'll pay you two million."

Cheung grinned. "I will be in touch."

Kiku, Daichi, and Jimmy walked back up the staircase to the top floor.

"He let us leave unescorted," Kiku noted.

"That's because last time you almost killed the short guy throwing him down the stairs," Jimmy said, now walking down a hall beside her. "Daichi, I can't believe you traded an entire shopping center for safe passage. And I thought the Jade Plaza was expanding."

"It was. But when they dug a couple of test holes, they found out the whole thing is sitting on a World War Two dump. Who knows what's buried there. If you think the Rat King hated Kiku before, wait until he finds out he's on the hook for the environmental cleanup fees." Daichi laughed. "I'll write the whole thing off as a loss and walk away with a million, and his men will be off our backs until we get out of town. Plus, Cheung won't be talking to Kenzo until after I sign those papers."

Kiku chuckled. "I never suspected you were such a savvy businessman."

Daichi winked. "I'm not just a pretty face."

Jimmy hung his head. "We still don't know where my sister is."

"For two million pounds, you can believe the Rat King is going to have his people scour the city," Daichi said, trying a little too hard to sound hopeful.

"And if they do not, we wait for the kidnappers to reach out to us," Kiku said as they exited the building. "Try calling her again."

Jimmy took out his phone and dialed. "I'll never be able to pay you back, Daichi. Two mill— Hello? Hello? Fumie?"

Kiku grabbed the phone, keeping it close to Jimmy's ear but angling it so she could hear.

"Your sister is safe," said a man who was clearly working to disguise his voice. "If you want her to stay that way, come alone to the Imperial Center across from Nan Lian Garden. Unit twelve. Bring ten thousand dollars, US."

"Wait! Let me speak with her! I want—"

The line disconnected.

Daichi clamped his hand down on Jimmy's shoulder. "I promise you, we'll get her back."

As soon as Jimmy turned away, Kiku caught Daichi's eye and made a slashing motion across her throat. He should never have promised Jimmy that. He couldn't.

For all they knew, Fumie was already dead.

and then. I would say it is not very likely, but it is possible. Daichi and I will go around the back and head in that way."

Jimmy shook his head. "They said, come alone."

Daichi scoffed. "They always say that. Look, Jimmy, you have to trust me."

"Have you ever dealt with a kidnapping?" Jimmy's foot was nervously tapping a rapid beat on the floorboard.

"At least a dozen." Daichi held up a hand. "Granted, in most of those situations I was the kidnapper, but I think that gives me a unique insight."

Kiku nodded.

Jimmy swore. "I never should have gotten her mixed up in this. This is my fault."

"It is," Daichi agreed.

Kiku pressed a sharp fingernail into his side.

"*But* ..." Daichi said, glaring at her, "you can try to fix your mistake now. If your sister isn't already dead."

Kiku rolled her eyes.

"What?" Daichi said innocently. "You told me to manage his expectations."

"You think she's dead?" Jimmy asked Kiku directly.

Kiku pressed her lips together. This conversation was going south fast, and she needed Jimmy to keep it together. "The longer we wait, the more that likelihood increases. You need to take the money to the door and let Daichi and me do what we do best. Can you do that, Jimmy?"

He nodded.

Daichi handed the gym bag back to Jimmy. "There's ten grand inside." They had picked up the money from an associate of Daichi's on the way. Apparently, ten thousand dollars was nothing to Daichi either.

"What do your sister and Doug look like?" Kiku asked.

Jimmy's eyes brimmed with tears. "Fumie has long dark hair. She's short—five two, I think. Doug is maybe six feet tall, with long blond hair he pulls back in a stupid-looking bun."

Daichi wrinkled his nose. "Maybe we should just rescue the sister."

Kiku punched his leg again.

"What? No!" Jimmy shook his head. "Get them both."

"I was kidding." Daichi rubbed his knee. "You know, gallows humor to lighten the mood. They use that in the US Special Forces."

"There are times when I think I should have honored Kenzo's request and brought him your tongue," Kiku said.

Daichi looked truly surprised. "Did my brother really ask you that?"

Kiku nodded.

"That's sick. I can't—"

"Stop!" Jimmy snapped. He opened the car door. "I gotta do this."

"Sorry," Daichi muttered.

"Close the door, Jimmy," Kiku said. "Let us get set up first. Give us five minutes and then go. Understood?"

Jimmy hesitated, then pulled the door closed. He looked ready to panic.

"You need to trust me, Jimmy. Do you?"

Jimmy's eyes searched hers. His fingers tightened on the strap on the gym bag. He nodded.

"Give me five minutes. Then go to the condo. Remember when you fell through the ice on the snowmachine?" I did not leave you then and I will not leave you now. Although you will not see me, I will be there watching out for you and your sister."

Jimmy nodded again, and Kiku and Daichi slipped out of the car.

It was still dark, but the rain had stopped. They crossed to a side street that ran behind the townhouses.

"What is wrong with you?" Kiku snapped.

"You told me to manage his expectations."

"I did no such thing. I specifically said, do not make promises like, 'We will get your sister back.' There is a big difference between not overpromising and saying things like"—she imitated his voice—"'She's probably dead.'"

"That's a pretty good impression of Sylvester Stallone if he smoked a dozen cigars a day."

Kiku shook her head. "I know as well as you do that Fumie is probably already dead. But we do not need Jimmy any more nervous than he already is. It was hard enough just getting him to agree to sit still for five min—" Kiku glanced back at the car and swore. "Jimmy's moving."

She and Daichi sprinted for the back of the townhouse. They

scaled a six-foot-high iron fence and dropped down into the small backyard, with mismatched outdoor furniture and a grill. Unit twelve was the only one with lights on, and it was lit up like a Christmas tree.

"I will take the second floor," Kiku said, eyeing the stout downspout.

Daichi smiled gratefully. "I'll go in the back door. Security system?"

"As they are expecting Jimmy to arrive, it is likely switched off. Let me go in the window first."

Kiku scurried up the metal downspout and leaned over to the closest window. From the desk, computer monitor, and bookshelf, the room inside appeared to be a home office, and it was unoccupied. She slid the window up and waited. Inside the house, downstairs, a TV set was playing. She gave a thumbs-up to Daichi, then slipped inside and drew her pistol.

Crouching low, she crept to the doorway and peered out into the carpeted hallway. There was another room to her left and a staircase on her right. Directly in front of her was a balcony that overlooked the living room.

Moving slowly, she snuck close to the banister and peeked over the side.

Tied to a chair in the middle of the living room was a small woman with long dark hair, wearing baggy casual clothes. She sat staring at the TV with a blank expression on her face, a bandana drooping around neck.

A man walked into the room, with a gun tucked into his waistband. He was tall, wearing a grey hoodie and sweatpants, and had his blond hair tied up in a bun.

"What are you doing?" the girl said. "Put your mask on."

"Relax. He's not here yet." The man walked to the window.

"He'll be here. Put your mask on."

"Listen, ten grand isn't enough. We should have asked for more."

The girl shook her head. "Jimmy doesn't have more than that. He's not a real gangster, he's a wannabe."

Kiku seethed, and her fingers tightened on the grip of her gun.

"Wannabe or not, Jimmy must've ticked off the wrong guy to get a price put on his head." Doug started to pace. "Maybe he ripped the

Yakuza off. You heard what Bunta said. They're offering a hundred grand. A *hundred grand*."

"What are you saying?" Fumie craned her neck to look at Doug, who stopped pacing. "I agreed to say I was kidnapped to help you get out of debt, but I can't give my brother up to the Yakuza. They might kill him."

"It's a hundred thousand dollars," said Doug.

Fumie scoffed. "There's *no way* they would give us that money for Jimmy."

Doug squatted down in front of her. "But they will, baby. They have to. It's like the code of the street or some stupid crap like that. That's how they work."

Fumie shook her head. "He's my brother."

"And *someone's* going to turn him in for the reward. Why not us? Think about it. You want to go back to school, right?"

Fumie exhaled.

"Jimmy got himself into this jam. You told him. You tried to warn him. Everyone in Hong Kong is looking for him."

"But he's coming here to help me."

"Because you're worth it." Doug brushed back her hair and smiled at her. "And we'll clear a hundred and ten thousand dollars. With that, we could really light up Tokyo Disneyland."

Fumie smiled.

Kiku raised her gun. She should blow the head off that heartless—

The doorbell rang.

"He's here," Fumie whispered excitedly.

Doug looked at her. "Are we agreed?"

Fumie nodded.

Doug kissed her, then lifted up a gag that had been around her neck to cover her mouth. He pulled on his ski mask. The bun made the back stand up. He looked ridiculous.

The doorbell rang again. Doug walked out of the living room and Kiku crept down the stairs. Fumie took one look at Kiku and started screaming, though her cries were muffled by the gag. Doug probably thought it was all part of the act.

Kiku heard the front door open, then Jimmy's voice.

you'll get over it. My father tried to have me killed and now my brother and my nephew both want to kill me, and I'm doing all right."

Kiku waited for them both to leave, then pressed the barrel of her gun against the top of Fumie's head. "You are his older sister. You had a sacred obligation to watch over him."

Fumie's whole body shook as she sobbed.

"You deserve death," Kiku said. "I want you dead. It will bother me at night knowing I let you live. But your brother has shown you mercy, and I will honor Jimmy's decision."

She then squatted down beside Doug and yanked his head up by his hair. When he opened his mouth to scream, Kiku jammed her pistol into his mouth.

Doug's eyes went wide.

"If either of you so much as breathe Jimmy's name ever again, I will make you beg for the comforts of the fires of Hell. *Do you understand?*"

Doug nodded.

Kiku took the gun out, the barrel rattling against Doug's teeth. He turned his head to the side and threw up.

Kiku stormed out of the room. They deserved to die. Both of them. Because of them, Kiku, Daichi, and Jimmy were all in Hong Kong.

And if the Rat King was true to form, Kenzo knew they were there, too.

16

It was almost four thirty in the morning as they started back toward the safe house, and between the rain and the hour, Hong Kong's streets were relatively empty. Kiku drove, Jimmy sat silently in the back seat sipping a large drink, and Daichi surfed on his phone.

"Here," Daichi said, holding his phone out so Jimmy could see. "Get one of these when it's over and you'll forget all your problems."

Jimmy looked at the screen and chuckled. "Maybe."

Kiku glanced at the screen. Daichi had pulled up a picture of a dozen puppies.

"You want one?" Daichi asked. "My neighbor just had a litter. Lilly texted me."

"No, thank you." Kiku turned down a side street to avoid the main road. "I am not home enough to keep a plant alive, let alone a dog. Although I have thought about it. My friend Jack has a king shepherd."

Jimmy sat forward. "What's a king shepherd?"

Kiku smiled. "Think German shepherd on super-soldier serum. Lady is one hundred and twenty pounds. She is a wonderful dog, but if you cross Jack or Alice, she will kill you."

"Sounds like you," Daichi joked.

Kiku scowled.

Daichi laughed. "Seriously, who is this Jack? You keep—"

The rear window shattered, Daichi's head jerked forward, and red spray covered the windshield.

Kiku stomped on the gas and cut onto another street, now veering back toward the main road. "Daichi?"

He didn't respond. He was pressed against the door with his head leaning on the window.

"Daichi!"

The car lost a hubcap as Kiku sped back onto the main road.

"One car. Huge SUV," Daichi said. He sat back up, wiping the red liquid from his face.

Kiku glanced back at Jimmy. He was staring out the broken back window, his gun in his right hand, his soda cup in his left. The cup had a giant bullet hole in it, red liquid dripping out of the side.

Jimmy tossed his cup out the broken window and held his gun in both hands. "Can I shoot at the SUV on the straightaway?"

"Move over," Daichi said. He clambered into the back. "I want to hit it, not just shoot at it."

Kiku sped around another vehicle. The driver laid on his horn, flipped her off, and held up his phone.

"The police will be here soon," Kiku said. "End this, Daichi."

Daichi fired three shots, then swore. "That should have killed the driver, but they didn't slow."

Kiku swore too. "Kenzo's personal cars all have bulletproof glass."

"I'll take out the tires." Daichi fired four more shots.

"They are self-sealing." Kiku pumped the brakes to avoid a car taking a right.

"When did my brother start taking such precautions?"

"When you went rogue."

Daichi grinned. "How are we going to stop it?"

"We will let the police figure that out. Get down." Kiku grabbed her phone and dialed.

"Nine-nine-nine emergency response," the operator answered in Cantonese.

Daichi's left eyebrow rose high while the other dropped. He mouthed, *Are you crazy?*

Jimmy nodded in agreement.

Kiku spoke in English, her voice rising dramatically. "My husband's gone insane! He's chasing me north down Mody Road. He's in a black SUV and he's *shooting* at me!" She screamed as she passed another car. "He's going to kill me! He has a gun!"

"Calm down, miss." The operator was now speaking English, too. "What is the make—"

Blue lights clicked on up ahead—a police car parked against the curb. "I see the police! I'm passing Minden Row. *Help!*" Kiku let out a loud fake sob before hanging up.

She blazed past the police car. The cruiser started to pull out behind her, but the SUV smashed right into its front corner panel, knocking the smaller car onto the sidewalk.

At the next intersection, Kiku cut the wheel hard, tires screeching. She clipped a Mini Cooper without slowing. "Get ready to jump out."

"Are we all getting out?" Daichi asked.

"No. You two need to get back to Takeo. I will draw them away. You can steal a car at the mall."

"I'm staying," Daichi said.

Jimmy nodded. "Me too."

Kiku held up her gun. "You are both mistaken if you think I was making a request. If I get pulled over, my story only makes sense if I am alone. When I slow down, jump."

Daichi scowled.

Jimmy whispered, "What do we do?"

Daichi whispered back, but loudly enough that Kiku would be sure to hear: "Do you remember when you thought Kiku was the type of person who would shoot you? She is. And she'd shoot me, too." He grabbed the door handle and raised his voice. "Because when she gets focused on a mission, nothing else matters!"

Kiku slammed on the brakes and turned sharply into an alley, just barely scraping between two metal posts set up to block off truck traffic. They lost both side mirrors, but they fit through.

"Get down!" she ordered as gunfire erupted behind them. Bullets pinged off the car.

They lost the front bumper as Kiku clipped the posts at the far end of the alley. Ignoring the cross traffic that had to grind to a halt, Kiku barreled across the street and shot into the next alley.

When she neared the end, she skidded to a stop. "Out."

Daichi and Jimmy jumped out, and Kiku hit on the gas. She turned hard to the right and headed for the heart of the city. Blue lights flashed in her rearview mirror. She stuffed her gun under her thigh, slowed down, and stuck her hand out the window, frantically pointing behind her.

The SUV exited the alley and appeared behind the police car. The lights on top of the cruiser shattered, sending glittering sparkles into the air. Some of the bullets made it through to Kiku's car. One lodged itself in the dashboard.

Kenzo must have lost his mind if he gave his men permission to shoot at the police.

Kiku yanked the wheel to the right and stomped on the gas. As she flew into the turn, the car leaned hard to the left—and when she straightened out, it still listed. The back left tire had been shredded, and the rim was sending sparks flying into the sky.

Kiku glanced back. She'd gained some distance on both pursuing vehicles. The police cruiser had crashed into a parked car, and the SUV had been going too fast to make the turn—though it would surely resume its pursuit momentarily.

She turned down the first side street and turned the car so it was blocking the road. Then she grabbed her gun, jumped out, and ran. Behind her, the SUV skidded and turned onto the street.

Kiku ducked into an alley and peered out. The SUV could have easily rammed her smaller car out of the way—and if she'd been driving the SUV that's what she would have done. But instead, the SUV stopped, and three men jumped out. Two men were still visible in the front seat, and they appeared to be speaking with someone else in the back seat.

At least six men.

Kiku had a double-stack Glock 19 with two magazines. Thirty bullets.

The SUV's tires spun as the driver backed out of the alley, and three buff and well-equipped men sprinted forward, eager for the hunt.

Kiku calmed her breathing and waited as footsteps echoed off the tar. She relaxed her fingers and forced herself to smile. It was a trick that Daichi had taught her. He'd pointed out that when people stiffen up, they slow down. In a fight, fast and accurate wins the day.

And she would never forget what he told her next: *Kill and have fun.*

The first man ran around the corner.

Kiku shot him in the head.

Time slowed as adrenaline swept through her. The two remaining men were caught completely off guard. Three rapid shots center mass dropped the second man, who held a machine gun. Momentum carried him past the entrance of the alley, his legs tangling together and his arms flailing as he fell.

The third man had a pistol. He was pulling the trigger as fast as he could, but the bullets were pinging off the ground as his arm hadn't caught up with his panicked brain.

It never would.

Kiku dropped him with three more shots. She had already turned and was five strides down the alley before his body landed on the tar.

Her magazine had only eight bullets left, and she instinctively swapped it out with a fresh one before putting the gun in her back holster. She slowed to a measured walk as she exited to the street.

Three men. Two seconds. Life was not cheap; she knew that better than anyone. But it certainly was fragile. No matter how much a vile act she knew taking a life was, she killed regularly and without hesitation.

Her breathing was calm as she strolled casually down the sidewalk. If she made it back to Takeo's, the first man she killed tonight would keep her awake—for a time. She could still picture his wide eyes and questioning gaze. But then she would sleep soundly. She would sleep as peacefully as a killer could. Because, in the fraction of a second before she pulled the trigger, his expression had changed, and in that moment she knew that he would have killed her if she had given him the chance.

17

Kiku thrust her hands into her pockets and crossed the street. The bus station was one block over. She could blend in with the people there, get a lift across the city, and double back to Takeo.

Sirens blared in the distance from several locations. No doubt the police were scrambling to cover the multiple crime scenes and traffic accidents she'd left in the wake of her one-woman crime wave.

A few people were out walking, even at this hour, and when two police cruisers screamed down the center of the street, followed by an ambulance, everyone stopped and gawked. Kiku did the same, as if she, too, were wondering what all the fuss was about.

At the next corner, a bus was picking up passengers. She hurried over and took her place in line—sandwiched between an elderly couple and two women cackling away about their plans to get the upper hand on one of their exes. She attempted to look bored, which wasn't much of a stretch. She wasn't worried about Daichi and Jimmy. Despite Daichi's prosthetic, which made him an easy read for pursuers, he was even better at stealing a vehicle than she was, and once he was in a car, he'd be invisible on the street.

When at last the line shuffled onto the bus, Kiku settled into an aisle seat next to a bleary-eyed businessman. Judging by the fumes of smoke and cheap whiskey wafting off him, she concluded he was heading home after an extremely late night. For everyone else on board, this was probably the early bus, not the late one.

The last passenger to board was a young man, probably a student, with a backpack. He pushed his glasses up his nose, scanned the rear of the bus for an empty seat, and frowned when he saw that the only free spots were up front, across from the two conspiring ladies.

The bus driver did a manual head count before sitting down and shutting the door. Kiku exhaled. But then someone pounded on the door. The driver opened it, and a thuggish-looking man in a long-sleeved shirt got on. The driver opened his mouth to say something, but a cross look from the man shut him down.

Scowling, the man grabbed the metal pole behind the driver and took his time studying each passenger. Kiku pretended to be examining her nails as she watched him. He rocked forward as the bus pulled away from the station, and Kiku caught a glimpse of the tattoo stretching up his neck from beneath his T-shirt.

"I wonder if he's going to stand the whole way," the businessman beside her whispered a little too loudly.

The thug glared at him, then his gaze shifted to Kiku. She met his stare just long enough to act frightened and flustered, then lowered her eyes. The thug flopped into the seat next to the student with the backpack. The student moved away as far as he could, shifting his backpack to between his feet.

Kiku covertly studied the new arrival. Black shoes, black pants, dark-gray shirt. She didn't see any telltale bulges, but she hadn't gotten a look at his back. The bus rounded a corner, and the student's backpack tipped over and touched the man's shoe. The older man swore loudly and kicked the backpack.

"I'm sorry." The student picked up the bag and placed it in his lap. A woman reached over and tapped his shoulder. When he looked back at her, she pointed to the luggage racks above the seats. "Thank you." The poor guy stood up and bowed. Holding the metal poles with one hand, he made his way down to an open spot in the rack near Kiku, and raised the backpack toward the rack. His shirt lifted, revealing a tattoo on his back.

Kiku leapt out of her seat just as the student spun around and swung the heavy backpack at her face. The backpack slammed against her empty seat. Kiku struck fast, aiming for his throat, but the young man was just as quick and blocked her strike.

The bus driver jammed on the brakes.

The older thug leapt to his feet with a gun in his hand. "Keep driving!" he ordered.

People screamed. Others cowered in their seats.

The student kicked at Kiku's shin, but she easily blocked the blow with her foot. She feigned a left jab and brought her right fist down on the bridge of his glasses, breaking his nose.

More people were screaming now, and the thug was waving the gun around, shouting for the bus driver to drive and the passengers to shut up—threatening to shoot everyone if both didn't happen immediately.

The student lunged at Kiku, a long-handled knife appearing in his right hand like a magician's trick card. Kiku twisted to the side, and the blade only nicked her forearm as she grabbed the man's wrist. The bus swerved, and they both swayed with it. It was like fighting on a seesaw.

Kiku waited for the bus to rock back, then she slammed her foot down on the student's instep, breaking the small bones there. He cried out, but Kiku was not finished with him yet. She brought his right arm toward her and drove his extended arm against the metal pole. More bones snapped, and the knife tumbled from his hand.

She spun the young man around toward the front of the bus and drew her gun. Placing one hand against the man's back, she used him as a shield as the older thug opened fire.

Two bullets hit the student before Kiku put a three-round burst into the thug. One of her bullets passed through him and shattered the front windshield.

The bus driver slammed on the brakes. Kiku grabbed the pole and managed to hang on, but the faux student shot forward and rolled to a heap in the front. The thug pitched backward and went right through the windshield. The bus lurched as its momentum sent it skidding right over his body.

Kiku hurried to the front of the bus, and the bus driver opened the door for her with a trembling hand. She hopped down, turned around, and gave him a slight nod.

"My apologies."

She then ran down the street and disappeared into the night.

19

Kiku knew something was wrong the minute she walked into the kitchen. Olivia and Daichi were talking in low voices next to the sink. Kiku couldn't make out their words, but Olivia's tone was strained. Daichi's face paled, and they both began to exit the room.

Kiku planted her feet. "Say it in front of me. What is wrong?"

Olivia glanced at Daichi, who nodded. "Takeo's fever has returned. It's very serious."

"How serious?" Kiku asked.

"Unless we take him to a hospital, he will die," Olivia said plainly.

"A hospital is not an option. What is the cause of his fever?"

Olivia glared. "You're not hearing me. Takeo has an infection. I suspect that foreign material is still in the wound. I understand you have a mission, but you are gambling with his life."

The muscles in Kiku's arm tightened. "If we bring Takeo to the hospital, the doctors will save him. But those same doctors, when offered enough money to pay for their college loans and children's tuition fees, will provide Kenzo with his son's location. And Kenzo will have Takeo killed."

"This infection is taking over. He *will* die if—"

"What medical equipment do you need?" Kiku asked. She was

annoyed with the woman but was even angrier with Daichi, who hovered close by, as if fearful Kiku would kill her.

"An ultrasound for starters. But I'll need a full medical bay so we can open him up and remove the source of the infection."

Daichi stepped in between the two women. "Kiku is right, no hospital. We need to think outside the box."

"Why can we not get Olivia what she needs and set up a sterile area here?" Kiku asked Daichi.

Olivia shook her head. "No. I can't operate on Takeo here."

"I'm not asking you to." A crooked smile spread across Daichi's face. "I know a place. Technically, it's a hospital, and it should have all the equipment you need."

"What do you mean, 'technically' it's a hospital?" Olivia crossed her arms.

"It's an animal hospital. I have a friend who's a vet."

Olivia looked back and forth between Daichi and Kiku like she was at a tennis match. "Are you serious?"

Daichi shrugged. "He's a high-end vet. But we need to find a covert ride to get Takeo there."

"I already asked Jimmy to get transportation," said Olivia. "He should have been back by now."

Music echoed faintly through the kitchen windows—a soft, playful tune that tickled their ears.

"What is that?" Daichi grumbled. He opened the back door.

An ice cream truck had pulled into the driveway, its music blaring and its lights making the surrounding houses glow.

Daichi ran outside, yanked open the driver's door, and flicked off both the lights and music. "What is wrong with you?" he snapped at Jimmy.

"What? You always see the ice cream truck with its lights and music on. I would have stuck out if they were off."

Daichi rubbed his temples with one hand. "You are a moron."

"Thanks." Jimmy rolled his eyes.

"Actually, he is a genius," Kiku said. "No one will suspect an ice cream truck, and it will keep Takeo cool. Time to move."

"I'll need a few minutes to get him ready to transport," Olivia said, heading back inside, Kiku on her heels.

When they were both in the kitchen, Olivia stopped and turned to face Kiku. Olivia's eyes narrowed, but her lip trembled. "If he doesn't make it ..." She inhaled sharply. "It's not on me. I am completely opposed to this."

"The responsibility for this decision is solely my own."

"No." Olivia's eyes welled up. "It's not. I could insist."

"I know you are a friend of Daichi's and you are a caring doctor. So please let me ease your conscience. If you insisted that we take Takeo to the hospital, we would still be going to the vet's office and you would still be operating on Takeo. The only difference would be my gun pressed against your head. Takeo's life is in my hands, not yours, Doctor."

Olivia closed her eyes and shook her head. She looked ready to say something more but instead turned and led Kiku into the living room.

Takeo's skin was mottled and his hair was matted with sweat. His sunken eye sockets were a sickly yellow-brown. Kiku was tempted to call an ambulance right that second—but she knew that was out of the question.

While Olivia gathered supplies, Kiku stayed at Takeo's bedside, softly stroking his arm, but remained silent. She had so much to say to him, but now was not the time.

When Jimmy and Daichi returned from prepping the truck, they moved Takeo onto the same backboard that they'd used to bring him into the house. He moaned weakly, his eyes opening and locking momentarily with Kiku's. She slipped her hand in his and gave it a reassuring squeeze.

Takeo tugged at Kiku's hand and opened his mouth as if to speak.

Kiku leaned over, nuzzling her head next to his.

"Saraba da," Takeo whispered.

She gasped at the sentimental phrase. His farewell sliced through Kiku's heart like a dagger. "Not today, Takeo. Your son needs you ..."

Takeo closed his eyes and his hand went limp. Kiku stood staring in sheer terror. "... I need you," she whispered in his unconscious ear.

"Let's move!" Daichi ordered, snapping her into action.

Soon they were all hunkered down in the ice cream truck. Jimmy drove carefully as the musical jingle played, but each bump made Takeo groan in pain, and the twenty-minute trip felt like forever. Kiku wished Takeo's infection were a human opponent she could annihilate. Against this invisible threat, she felt helpless.

Jimmy parked behind the veterinary hospital, and they carried Takeo inside. They were greeted by an older Japanese man with a scarred face. Daichi had told them the doctor was a burn victim and his face had been heavily reconstructed. Kiku would have had a difficult time meeting his gaze were it not for his kind eyes, enlarged by his thick glasses.

"Kiku, Olivia, Jimmy, this is Shu."

The vet bowed low to Daichi, then turned to Olivia. "I have the room all prepped. I will need you to assist me."

"Were you able to get any blood?" Daichi asked him.

"Yes. Plasma, too. My brother works at the hospital."

"Tell him I am in his debt."

Shu smiled ruefully. "He'd kill me if he knew I was helping you."

As they walked to the operating room, a dog barked from a room down the hallway, which sparked a chain reaction among the other animals. They stepped through the entrance and moved into the large room, which was meticulously clean, the various tool and appliances stored neatly away in their holders.

"You'll have to forgive the noise," the vet said. He led Olivia to a surgical scrub sink while the others placed Takeo on a stainless-steel operating table in the middle of the room.

Olivia brought Shu up to speed on Takeo's condition, then Shu examined Takeo's wound. When he pressed gently on Takeo's side, Takeo winced.

"Let's take a look with the ultrasound," the vet said.

They wheeled the machine over to Takeo, and everyone shifted over to view the monitor. Shu wiped the area around the wound with alcohol, then applied a cool gel before touching the scanner to Takeo's skin. Takeo moaned and shifted.

"We need him to lie still," said the vet. "Would you hold his shoulders and legs?"

Daichi moved to hold Takeo's shoulders, and Kiku pinned his legs. Shu then moved the scanner over the wound again and again. When Takeo's arms started to rise, Jimmy and Olivia stepped in to keep them still.

Takeo's eyes snapped open. He glared up at Jimmy. "You're a dead man!" he screamed. Then his head flopped to the side and he passed out.

Jimmy looked back and forth between Kiku and Daichi. "He's delirious, right? You'll explain I was just helping, won't you?"

Shu pointed at the monitor. "There."

The dark spot on the monitor confirmed Kiku's worst fears. Dr. Ito had indeed missed something when he'd removed the bullet.

Olivia nodded. "We need to get it out."

Shu made several markings on Takeo's abdomen with a marker, then he and Olivia stepped out to dress for surgery.

As the others waited, Daichi leaned down and placed his forehead against Takeo's. Daichi closed his eyes and his lips moved. She couldn't hear what he said, but as he finished, he whispered, "Amen."

Shu and Olivia returned wearing surgical scrubs, hats, and masks. Shu motioned to the hallway. "We will need all of you to step out. You will be able to observe through the glass."

Kiku, Daichi, and Jimmy exited, and Olivia and Shu moved over to the table. As they worked, the two doctors spoke in calm tones. If Kiku didn't know better, she would have assumed they'd worked together before. After several minutes, they both smiled triumphantly as Shu pulled a circular plug of fabric out of Takeo's chest cavity.

"Got it!" He held it in the air for them to see.

A doorbell rang.

Looking startled, Shu pointed to the front of the building. "That's the front door."

Kiku hurried down the hallway and peeked around the corner. Two policemen stood just outside the entrance. She raced back to the operating room.

"There are two policemen at the front door."

Shu glared at the ceiling. "We had a break-in a few weeks ago. If I don't go ..."

"Go," Olivia said. "I can close him up."

Shu bowed and hurried out of the room, removing his surgical mask and gown.

"Kiku, you need to assist me," Olivia said.

Kiku shook like she'd been Tased. "Me? No."

Daichi held up his prosthetic. "Well, it obviously can't be me. And do you really want Jimmy playing doctor?"

"Now!" Olivia snapped. "Put on a gown and wash your hands. Thoroughly."

Kiku took a surgical gown from the wall and slipped into it, then washed her hands at the sink and joined Olivia in the operating room. The sight of blood had never bothered her before, but now that it was Takeo's, it upset her to no end.

"Put these gloves on and grab that sponge. Do everything I say." Olivia's calm, even tone was just what Kiku needed, but she could not stop her hands from shaking, which made her angry. Her hands were always rock steady. Always. Yet now she looked like a meth addict detoxing. And she literally had Takeo's blood on her hands.

At one point, Takeo drew a ragged breath, and his whole body shuddered. Kiku gazed down at his handsome face. *Wake up, damn it!* she wanted to scream. She wondered if she would ever feel his touch again.

After a few more minutes, Shu came back, pulling on a mask. "Bad time to drop by for a visit. The police were just following up on the break-in. But I know those officers from my involvement with their K9 dogs. They will not be an issue." He scrubbed up and took over for Kiku.

Kiku peeled off the bloody gloves, threw them in the trash, and practically ran out into the hallway. She must be sick, that was it. Maybe something she ate. She wiped her cheek and stared at her trembling hands in disbelief. She didn't even recognize them as her own. She clenched one hand into a fist and pulled her arm back, ready to take her anger out on the wall. But Daichi grabbed her arm.

"Easy," he said. "Keep it together, kid."

Kiku was ready to punch him instead. She snarled, "Get off me! I am fine. It is just ..." She trailed off as a tear rolled down Daichi's face. She'd never seen him cry.

Daichi exhaled. "When my first wife died ... Takeo was just a kid then. He rode his bike thirty miles to bring me a puppy." He hung his head. "It was his own dog. Kenzo said if he gave it to me, he'd never give him another one. Takeo did it anyway." He looked at the doors to the operating room, then nodded as if he'd reached a conclusion. "Whether Takeo lives or dies, I promise you this: I'm going to kill Kenzo."

Kiku shook her head. "No. *I* will kill him first."

20

Kiku and Jimmy waited in the hall while Olivia and Shu finished up with Takeo. Daichi stood a short distance away, talking on his phone.

"You don't think Takeo's going to remember what he said when he woke up, do you?" Jimmy asked nervously.

"No," Kiku said. "Let it go."

"Easy for you to say. He didn't threaten to kill *you*." Jimmy walked over to a soda machine. He stuck two bills into the machine and smacked a button. Nothing happened. "Oh, come on." He jammed the button down repeatedly, then stepped back, ready to rock the machine.

"Stop it," Kiku said.

"If I didn't have bad luck, I'd have no luck at all." Jimmy thrust his hand into his pocket and frowned. "Great. That's the last of my cash."

Kiku reached out and held the button down. The machine rumbled, and his soda appeared at the bottom. "There is no such thing as luck. You are too impulsive. It causes mistakes."

"I might be a moron on occasion, but I am *not* a child. How was I supposed to know you had to hold the stupid button down?"

"It is common sense. The machine is old, so the switches are worn down. You need to observe at all times, even when you feel anxious. Details will tell you a story, if you let them speak." Kiku brushed her dark hair away from her face and tucked it behind her ear. "For example, you panicked on the lake and nearly drowned. Luck was not your issue that day, but a lack of self-mastery of your emotions. Now you are getting all worked up about something Takeo said while semiconscious. He was barking at the wind and will have no recollection of what he said. Make your own luck, Jimmy."

Jimmy opened his soda and took a swig. His brows knitted together. "Okay. I'll give you that much. But what about my sister turning on me? How was that not bad luck?"

Kiku shrugged. "When you are dealing with people, it is more complicated. You have said you had bad parents. That increased the chances that your sister would follow their example. Your sister obviously made a poor choice in choosing her scumbag husband over her loyal brother. Again, I believe in bad decisions, not luck."

Shu and Olivia exited the operating room. Their expressions were neither grim nor encouraging. Kiku motioned for Daichi to get off his phone and come over, but he held up his prosthetic, indicating he would join them in a minute.

"All of Takeo's vital signs look favorable," Olivia said. "He lost very little blood, which is good, but he still has to fight off the infection." Concern was etched on her tired face. "We have started a combination of powerful antibiotics that we are administering intravenously. It will take several hours to complete the first round. It's in his best interest to remain here for further IV treatment."

Kiku shook her head. "He comes with us."

"You'll kill him," Olivia snapped.

"Hold on," Shu said timidly. "I will personally assure his safety while he is in my care."

"It is not you I am concerned with, Doctor." Kiku gave the man a slight bow. "All of Japan knows of the bounty on Takeo's head. You have staff, and there would be people coming in."

"The staff is my family. Literally. My son is my assistant and my daughters run the front. We have a quarantine room in the back. And Olivia has already agreed to stay here and watch over Takeo."

"If he stays, it is I who will watch over him," Kiku said firmly.

"I'm afraid that's not possible," Daichi said. He walked up, stuffing his phone in his pocket. "We have to go."

The look on his face told Kiku everything she needed to know. Daichi's men had located Kenzo.

"Then Jimmy stays here," Kiku said.

"What? No. I don't want to get left behind," Jimmy protested.

"You will watch Takeo."

"I mean no offense," Shu said softly, like he was dealing with an injured animal, "but Olivia can blend in here. Jimmy ... would not."

Daichi raised a hand. "Excuse us one moment." He motioned for Kiku to follow him down the hall, out of earshot of the others.

"I do not like this," Kiku whispered. "We cannot leave Takeo undefended."

"If Kenzo's men discover that Takeo is here, the vet will deal with it."

"Him?" Kiku scoffed. "He's a sweet man, but—"

"He's Shigeru."

The words shocked her as much as a slap in the face. Shigeru had been Daichi's brother-in-arms. Daichi had been known as "Demon" and Shigeru as "Death." Brothers from Hell.

"You're not the only one who can fake a person's death," Daichi continued. "Shigeru and I, and now you, are the only ones who know. Even his kids are unaware of the truth."

Kiku resisted the urge to glance back down the hallway. She could not ask for better security than Shigeru, but ...

"What is there to debate?" Daichi leaned in. "He's almost as good as me."

"*Almost* does not inspire confidence."

Daichi smiled. "Yes, almost. And it's only because I lost a hand that it's even close. But we don't have a lot of time. I'm taking the ice cream truck to the airport. Are you coming with me?"

The debate was over. There was no choice. In order to protect the man she loved, she'd have to leave his side to go after his father, one of the most dangerous men alive.

21

Parked along a side street, Daichi and Kiku sat in the front seat of car while Jimmy sat in the back. Kiku balanced her laptop on the dashboard.

"Kenzo has a shipping business near Noshiro Port. He has a small home there," Daichi said, pointing at the image on the laptop.

"I know of it," said Kiku. "You are certain he is there?"

"Positive."

Jimmy shook his head. "If you think that's a small house, I'd hate to see what you think is big. The place is a mansion."

"More like a fortress," said Daichi. "Gated. Guarded. High security." He scrolled the image until two tall buildings came into view. "These are the shipping offices. Workers are there till very late."

"Not anymore," Kiku said. "Kenzo moved the offices of the shipping company. He still owns the buildings, but he relocated the offices to Noshiro proper. Why are you interested in these buildings?"

"They're four stories tall. I have seen the rooftops from Kenzo's courtyard garden."

Kiku smiled. "Which means we can see into the garden from the rooftops. Excellent." She scrolled the footage so they were facing the house, with the buildings at their backs. But the only available view was at street level and completely obscured by trees. “You are thinking of a sniper shot?”

Daichi nodded. “My brother is an animal. I will put him down like one.”

“We need a dry run. It all depends on whether we have a line of sight.”

“What do I do?” Jimmy asked.

“Extraction.” Daichi pointed at the docks at the rear of the building. “I’ll take the building on the right, Kiku gets the left. Whoever has a clear shot takes it, and we’re gone. Easy.”

Jimmy shook his head. “Nothing is ever *easy*.” He looked at Kiku and said, “You were going to say that, right?”

Daichi exhaled and rubbed his eyes.

Kiku turned slowly to face Jimmy. “Are you mocking me?”

“No.” Jimmy held up his hands. “It’s just that ... I thought ... You know, the whole *there is no luck*. So, I thought ... I’m going to shut up now.”

“That’s the best idea you’ve had yet.” Daichi clapped him on the back.

Kiku replied, “It is true I do not believe in luck. And right now we need to make a list of supplies, including guns and climbing equipment.”

“You’re going to climb up the building?” Jimmy asked.

“No,” said Kiku, “but we will come down that way. We can have a rope over the edge in seconds, compared to minutes taking the stairs.”

“And seconds count,” added Daichi. “When do you want to conduct the recon?” he asked her.

“As soon as we get all the supplies. And who knows, if the opportunity presents itself, our scouting mission could go live.”

“Agreed,” Daichi said. “Jimmy will get the boat.”

Jimmy grinned. “The harbor is loaded with boats. It’ll be no problem stealing one.”

Kiku inhaled. “For the dry run, please rent one, and use a fake ID.”

“Right.” Jimmy nodded emphatically. “I’ve got one question. How many men do you think are protecting Kenzo?”

Daichi shrugged. “Three or four ...”

Jimmy was clearly relieved. "Great!"

"He's being sarcastic," Kiku said dryly. "There will be at least two dozen."

Jimmy's smile vanished.

Daichi laughed. "Don't worry. Kiku will handle most of them for us."

As soon as Daichi had parked the car behind the deserted office buildings, Kiku powered down the passenger window and launched the drone. Using her phone, she guided the drone up to the nearest roof. After rotating it three hundred sixty degrees to sweep for cameras, she flew it to the far edge, for a perfect, clear view of Kenzo's garden.

Daichi smiled, but it quickly faded. He pointed at her phone screen. "Can you zoom in?"

"Not until I get the drone back."

"Take a picture and bring it back."

Kiku photographed the garden, then flew the drone back across the roof. Daichi tapped his prosthetic against the steering wheel as she brought the drone back to the car. She removed the memory chip, slipped it into her laptop, and blew up the photo.

Daichi nodded. "That's it. He's here. We need to go *now*. No dry run. Call Jimmy."

"Hold on a second. What are you seeing?" Kiku examined the photograph herself. Two men were walking in the garden. One was carrying a large, round object while the other held a tray.

"That's Saki and Mato," Daichi said. "Kenzo is getting ready for archery. I'm certain of it."

Kiku remembered Kenzo shooting in his garden when he had tasked her with rescuing Jiro. "I will greenlight Jimmy. Grab your gear."

Daichi got out and opened the trunk, and Kiku called Jimmy and explained the situation. He'd already rented a boat and was moving into place.

"Is there anything else I can do for you guys?" Jimmy asked.

"Just make sure you are in place when I give the signal. Put your mic on and keep it on. We will do a test when we are in position on the roof."

As Kiku got out of the car, Daichi was already starting for the far building. He turned around and flashed her a big smile. "I get the first shot." Then he sprinted away.

Kiku knew Daichi wasn't eager to kill his brother. He was sick of killing. That was why he'd left the Yakuza. But she understood why he wanted to take the shot.

He would kill Kenzo so Kiku didn't have to.

So she wouldn't have to kill Takeo's father.

It was a noble gesture, but a pointless one. Takeo understood his father was a vicious fiend, wicked through and through. He would never hold it against her if she pulled the trigger.

Kiku grabbed her two duffel bags, closed the trunk, and ran to the rear door of her building. She picked the lock easily and slipped inside. The place had been mostly cleaned out, and it stank of decay and mold.

She found the stairway and took the cement steps two at a time. Daichi might already be assembling his sniper rifle and scoping in on Kenzo's head. And she wanted to beat him to it.

The door to the roof was rusted shut, but three well-placed kicks busted it open. She rushed to the edge of the roof, dropped her bags, and started to hook up her escape. The getaway plan always came first.

She tied the rappelling rope to an air-conditioning unit, attached a carabiner, and tossed the rope over the edge facing the docks. Then she returned to her bags, pulled out the sniper rifle, and slapped it together so quickly her hands were a blur. When she was done, she clicked her mic.

"Done."

"How was your nap?" Daichi quipped.

"Shut up. You can't be set up yet."

"Sure am."

Kiku heard the smile in his voice and knew he was telling the truth.

"I was right, too. Kenzo is coming out for archery practice. Are you seeing what I'm seeing?"

Kiku pressed her eye against the sight. The garden was now empty, but a few things had been set up. A table with a cup and a bottle on it. A target. And Kenzo's old-fashioned Japanese bow and quiver, which she recognized immediately.

Her breathing sped up. This was happening. Kenzo was about to die.

"I will take the shot," she said. "I appreciate your offer and I understand why you are doing it, but I am the better shooter."

"Ha!" Daichi laughed. "I've taught you a lot, but I'm still a better shot. Hell, I bet Alex can outshoot you now."

"Please tell me that you did not teach the boy how to shoot a gun."

"Every child needs to know how to shoot."

"I thought you were going the Christian route. What happened to beating swords into plowshares?"

"That's in Heaven, Kiku. Here, you still need a sword every once in a while. That's why Christ told his apostles to sell their cloaks and buy one."

"I do not want the boy to follow in his father's footsteps. Takeo is trying to leave that life behind, too."

"Takeo is still leading the Yakuza. It's kind of hard to leave that life behind when you're wrapped up in it."

"Takeo is trying to make the Yakuza a legitimate business organization," Kiku countered, her anger building. "That takes time."

Daichi exhaled into the mic. "Fine. But I am taking the shot. I don't care if you're sleeping with Takeo. This goes beyond that."

"What?" Jimmy's voice came over Kiku's earpiece. "You and Takeo are going at it?"

Daichi started laughing, but Kiku fumed. She valued her privacy, as did Takeo his. She would definitely take this up with Daichi later. She remained focused on the scene below when a door at one side of the garden opened. Two guards stepped out, and Kenzo walked through a moment later.

"Wait for him to launch the arrow," Daichi instructed. "We'll have a clear shot."

"Jimmy," Kiku said, her voice chilled, "go to the docks."

"On it," Jimmy said.

In an Armani suit, Kenzo strolled down the peastone path like he didn't have a care in the world. The two guards shadowed him, their heads on a swivel, scanning for threats.

"Hold ..." Daichi cautioned.

Kiku braced her rifle against the ledge of the building and forced herself to relax. The garden was a quarter mile away. It was a long shot, but she wouldn't miss.

Kenzo stopped at the table. One of the men poured him a cup of sake.

"Wait for it," Daichi whispered. "I have a clear line of sight."

"Me too." Only Kiku's mouth moved as she spoke. Other than that, she was a statue.

Kenzo sipped the drink and powdered his hands. He took his time picking up the bow and selecting an arrow.

Kiku's finger rested on the trigger. "I have the shot."

"Wait. I want to make certain."

One of the guards turned and looked toward the building Kiku was in.

"I am taking the shot," she said.

Kenzo released the arrow. It struck just below the target's red circle.

"Don't shoot!" Daichi ordered.

But it was too late. Kiku pulled the trigger. And all hell broke loose.

22

Kiku's bullet hit Kenzo square in the back of the head. And at the moment he pitched forward, she realized why Daichi had told her not to shoot.

Kenzo's arrow had missed the bull's-eye.

A memory flashed in her mind. She had seen Kenzo practicing with the bow and arrow at Takeo's summer home. The real Kenzo never missed. She'd been duped by a lookalike.

Hidden among the trees, three 50-caliber machine-gun nests opened fire on Kiku's position. The wall where she had leaned her sniper rifle disintegrated as she scrambled backward. She landed hard on her side and lost her earpiece. Holes appeared in the roof as bullets punched their way right through.

While Kiku crouched behind the air-conditioning unit, a hail of steel rained up at her, filling the air with a sound like a thousand angry bees. Almost a full minute passed before the shooting stopped.

Huge chunks of the roof were now gone. The short wall circling the roof of the building was reduced to rubble. Even the air-conditioning unit had holes ripped through it. It was a miracle that she had not been struck.

"Brother!" Daichi called out. "Hello!"

Kiku could practically hear the smile in his voice.

She looked at the building next door and was surprised to see him standing up, his sniper rifle in his left hand. He walked right up to the edge and tossed the weapon over the side.

"I bet you're surprised to see me!" he shouted.

A car door opened and closed somewhere near the rear of the building. Then the real Kenzo yelled back, "I'll deal with you shortly, Daichi."

The 50-calibers opened up on Kiku's position once more. She curled up in the fetal position as the shots pulverized the roof around her. Rock splinters sliced her skin, but the bullet she expected to strike miraculously never did.

The guns fell silent.

"Hey! I'm offended. Seriously," said Daichi. "I thought you hated me more than anyone on the planet, yet you keep shooting at *her*. And the reward for Kiku was twice what mine was!"

"You are history," Kenzo shouted back. "Permanently discarded to the past. Irrelevant. And truthfully, why would I waste my time on you? Father was right. You showed your true colors when you ran away. You never were a true Nakumora."

"Yeah. About that ..." Daichi chuckled. "You didn't want to kill Takeo because you wanted the one-hundred-percent-pure Japanese bloodline of the Nakumoras to continue." He rolled his head from side to side. "Well ... it's kind of too late for that."

Kiku sat up.

"I mean ..." Daichi shrugged. "Come on, Kenzo. Haven't you ever wondered why Takeo and Jiro look so much like *me*? You must have had some suspicions. It was not honorable what I did, but I am proud to be a father. They're *my* sons."

Kiku wished she could have seen the look on Kenzo's face. She couldn't, but everyone heard him scream. Kiku couldn't make out his words, or if they even were words—perhaps they were merely expressions of incoherent anger. But she understood his intent. And so did the men with the machine guns, who opened up on Daichi. The bullets ripped into the roof where Daichi was standing, and he disappeared in a cloud of debris.

Kiku ran for the other edge of the roof, clipped her carabiner to the one already attached to the rope, and plummeted over the side. Daichi had distracted Kenzo in an effort to protect her.

The ground rushed up at her, and she pulled the brake. Her harness cut into her sides and groin—she was gnashing her teeth to keep from crying out in pain—and her knees smashed into her chin as she tucked and rolled to absorb the impact.

She unclipped her harness in one fluid motion and came up running, but she didn't run for the safety of the boat. She raced around the far side of the building to flank the guns that were now focused on Daichi.

The two men in the first machine-gun nest never saw death coming. She shot both in the head and jumped behind their gun. In an instant she had it swiveled around, aimed at the next machine-gun nest. At that moment the two men stopped firing and started cheering. She could not drive from her mind the idea that there was only one explanation for their behavior—they believed Daichi was dead.

Was he? And had he been telling the truth? Was he Takeo's father, and Jiro's as well?

She held down the trigger as she raked the gun back and forth. The men in the third and last machine-gun nest finally realized there was a problem. They pivoted their weapon to face her. Kiku lined up her shot and opened fire first. Her bullets shredded them both.

Finally, she scanned for Kenzo. He was nowhere in sight, but a black SUV was barreling down the road toward his compound. She opened fire. Round after round slammed into the SUV, but it didn't even slow, and within seconds it was out of sight.

Kiku grabbed an M4 assault rifle and extra magazine from the hands of one of the dead men at her feet, leapt out of the machine-gun nest, and sprinted toward the docks.

She'd taken only a few steps when small-arms fire erupted from the direction of the house. But it wasn't targeting her. The target was Daichi's building. Which meant ...

He was still alive.

She looked up. Sure enough, there he was, at the edge of the roof. He had survived. But he wouldn't survive much longer. Every man on the ground was shooting at him.

Kiku broke a major rule: she fired only once at each target. There were simply too many men and too few bullets for her to fire in bursts. Every time she pulled the trigger, she saw a man fall. And still bullets kept flying up at Daichi.

He leapt off the roof and plunged toward the ground like a rag doll. Fast. Too fast. He needed to brake. *Why isn't he braking?*

And then Kiku saw the reason. Daichi was frantically trying to work the brake, but his prosthetic hook wouldn't fit inside the carabiner.

She had killed her mentor. The wound she had given him all those years ago was now going to be his undoing. She never should have gone after him in the first place. She had only done so because Kenzo had convinced her that Daichi had flipped—that he had gone to the FBI and was setting Takeo up. So Kiku chased him down with a fire in her gut that rivaled that of Paul the Apostle. She chased him down and fought the man who'd been a father to her. She battled him until he was beaten.

And then ... she didn't stop. She couldn't. Hate drove her like she was possessed. Even when she took away his hand, it wasn't enough.

Only when she was about to take his head did she realize that this was what Daichi had wanted all along. He *wanted* Kiku to win. And he wanted his death to look good—for her sake. Because Kenzo had suspected that she was following her master in rebellion.

If Daichi did not die ... Kenzo would kill Kiku, too.

Kiku spared Daichi's life that day—because he had spared her life first. Together they faked his death, to end Kenzo's wrath.

Daichi had been a second father to Kiku.

And now ... she would be the cause of his death. Because her rage had taken his hand. Too late she was realizing who was truly on her side.

Daichi's body hit the ground with a sickening thud.

23

Kiku couldn't see where Daichi had fallen—a hedgerow obscured her view—but she ran toward the spot all the same. She paused at the hedges, gunfire crackling around her, and pressed the M4 against her cheek. Targeting a group of three men, she quickly took down two of them, then was startled when the third man's head snapped back before she could fire.

That bullet had come from the docks.

Jimmy.

She moved forward cautiously while maintaining a steady pace. Two cars had stopped near the corner of the building, and several of Kenzo's men were using the cars for cover. She spotted what they were shooting at. Jimmy was pinned down behind a huge electrical box, with Daichi at his feet. Daichi's legs were twisted at odd angles and his face was hardly recognizable because of the pain, but he was alive.

Kiku had three bullets left in her magazine. She unloaded those and swapped in a fresh one. "Move! I will cover you!" she shouted, and she opened fire, forcing the men to take cover behind their cars.

Jimmy grabbed Daichi by his climbing harness and started dragging him toward the dock. Kiku moved steadily sideways as she covered Jimmy. Daichi was firing, too, even as he was dragged. Between the two of them, they kept their enemy pinned down.

Somehow Jimmy managed to get to the dock before Kiku's M4 clicked on an empty chamber. She turned and raced to catch up.

"That could have gone better," Daichi groaned as Kiku grabbed the other side of his vest and helped Jimmy lift him into the boat. Daichi swore nonstop, and at one point Kiku truly feared that he was going to bite her.

As bullets pinged off the railings of the dock, Kiku jumped behind the wheel and hit the throttle. Ducking low, she glanced back to make sure Jimmy was on board. He'd collapsed into a seat, his face pale and covered in sweat, and he was starting to shake.

"Jimmy!" Kiku shouted. "You need to put pressure on your wound. Put your hand on it."

Jimmy moaned. "I don't think I can." He lifted his left arm slightly and winced. "I got hit on both sides. Left forearm, right shoulder."

"We will be back to the car in no time." Kiku tried to give him a reassuring smile. "But I need to look at your wounds *now*."

She couldn't leave the wheel for long—Noshiro Port was a brackish lake, and the water was choppy—but she throttled back the engine, rushed back to Jimmy, and helped him to the seat next to the wheel. After throttling back up and making a minor course correction, she grabbed the medical kit.

Both of Jimmy's gunshot wounds appeared to be through-and-throughs. The one in his left forearm had gone through the meat, and the blood flow was already slowing down. The one in his right shoulder had also missed bone.

"You could not have been shot in better locations."

"I'd like to have not been shot at all," Jimmy groaned. "You're saying it's not that bad? Because it sure feels bad."

"The bullet went through just below your collarbone and out the back. You will live." She packed gauze into the wound even as she steered the boat for the far shore.

"What are we going to do to help Daichi?" Jimmy asked. He looked back at Daichi's twisted legs.

Kiku took out her phone. "We are getting out of Japan. He needs a doctor, and so do you."

"What about Kenzo?"

Kiku smiled, but the news left a bitter taste in her mouth. She needed Daichi now, not in six months.

The door to Daichi's room opened and a nurse came out. Her cheeks were flushed bright red. "He's ready to see you now," she said in Russian before walking away.

Albert gently touched Kiku's arm. "I'll wait right here."

"Thank you." She smiled and entered Daichi's room.

"Can you believe this?" Daichi grumbled. Both of his legs were in thick casts and suspended by cables in traction. "And can you apologize to that nurse?" He pointed to the door. "I thought she was here for my sponge bath. I swear I wasn't trying anything."

Kiku raised an eyebrow.

Daichi held up his left hand and wiggled his wedding ring. "Happily married. I would never do anything to hurt Lilly. Speaking of which, there is no way I can stay here for six months."

"Agreed. I am going to take you home. But I have a favor to ask."

Daichi crossed his arms and waited.

"It would be safer for Jimmy and Takeo to go with you, too."

Daichi rolled his eyes. "You are aware that Alex and Hwan are living at my farm right now, right?"

"That is not my fault."

"Really? *Really?* Seems to me that I remember you brought both of them there."

Kiku sighed. "I have effectively screwed up your life."

"That's a fair assessment. But ... what happened at Noshiro wasn't your fault."

Kiku shook her head. "I never should have taken the shot."

Daichi grabbed her hand and gave it a squeeze. "Don't beat yourself up over a decision. Although ... I would have ... waited." He smiled. "My brother is many things, but a poor archer is not one of them."

Kiku chuckled and squeezed his hand back.

"Thank you for saving my life." She cleared her throat. "On the roof ... what you said to Kenzo. Was that the truth?"

"What? No." Daichi shook his head. "I was just trying to rile my brother. And it sure worked!"

Kiku let go of Daichi's hand and touched the cable suspending his legs.

"Careful ..." Daichi said. He reached out for her, but she easily moved out of the way.

"I need the truth from you." She strummed the cable like a cord on a harp.

Daichi winced. "I told you." He was looking worried. "I lied."

"Then or now?" Kiku strummed the cable harder this time. "Because Takeo has your eyes. So does Alex." She seized the cable. "I am going back to Japan to get Takeo. I need to know."

"Okay. Okay." Daichi held up his hand. "I told you about Kenzo and Itsumi. He was obsessed with producing an heir, and when she didn't get pregnant, he very nearly beat her to death. I figured it was only a matter of time before he succeeded. She was scared and had no one else to turn to. She begged me. And the truth is ... I loved her. It was wrong, but in a way ..." He shook his head. "No. I know it was still wrong." His hand balled into a fist. "And then Kenzo treated Jiro's mother the same way. I figured if it had worked once ..." He exhaled and glared at the ceiling. "They are my sons, and they're going to hate me."

"Not Takeo. He will be relieved that he is not related to that cruel and wicked man."

"Do you have any idea what kind of man I am?" Daichi tried to sit up. "I've killed way more men than Kenzo. I'm just a different kind of beast."

"Would a beast have taken Baba and four others into his home? Or saved me?"

"Saved you? I hate to break it to you, kid, but it might have been more merciful if I'd let them kill you when you were a child. Look at us. How many men did you just kill?"

Kiku thought for a moment. The truth was, she had no idea.

"I don't know how many either. Who in their right mind doesn't know how many people they've killed?" Daichi shook his head. "Did you know I tried to talk to a therapist once? Only a few minutes in, he gave me my money back—along with someone else's phone number."

Kiku waited several moments before speaking. "Is your pity party over?"

Daichi held up his prosthetic in a way that suggested it would have been an obscene gesture if he still had a hand.

"Your question was intended to be rhetorical," Kiku said, "but I have an answer to it. Warriors. Warriors often do not know how many they have killed in battle. War is an ugly business. You and I are warriors." Kiku's dark eyes met Daichi's, now brimming with tears. "I do not have much time before I leave for Japan. Albert is making arrangements. I will bring Takeo to your farm and meet you and Jimmy there."

"Look, Kiku. It's over." Daichi pointed at his broken legs. "Everyone else is out of commission. We're all going to have to go underground, hunker down, and hide."

Kiku looked out the window, but it was dark outside, so her reflection looked back at her. She knew they couldn't go underground for long. Kenzo was relentless, powerful, and cruel. Eventually, he would find and slaughter them all.

"I'm sorry about what I said," Daichi said. He tapped his chest. "I meant *I'm* a monster. Not you."

Kiku's reflection seemed to grow darker, her eyes black and her cheeks sunken. She wanted to run outside and embrace that darkness, let it wrap around her. She felt safe in the dark, at home in the night. She pressed her lips together ruefully, but in her reflection she seemed to be smiling.

Daichi was right. She was a monster. And monsters don't hide, they hunt.

25

As Kiku walked toward the front door of the animal hospital, a woman in her twenties was just coming out. She saw Kiku, smiled, and held the door open.

Kiku read her name badge. Sara, Shigeru's younger daughter.

"Is your father in?"

"He's running an errand. But your friends are waiting for you. I'll take you to the back."

"Thank you."

They passed Shigeru's two other children at the reception desk—Niko, the elder daughter, with bright-red dyed hair, and Touma, the son, with a stud earring in his left ear. They waved as Sara and Kiku passed. Both had their father's kind eyes.

"My father has arranged for transportation to the airport," Sara said. As they crossed in front of the kennels, four large German shepherds began barking ferociously, and Sara laughed. "And it's a good thing you're leaving today. These four are very, very loud. They're going to be used for stadium security. They have to be quarantined first and technically should be in individual cages, but since our quarantine room is occupied by your friend, we had to improvise."

They stopped outside the door to the quarantine room, and Kiku bowed. "I thank you and your family for your generosity."

Sara waved her hand dismissively. "Not a problem. My father helps everyone. I'll let you know when he gets here." She walked back to the front, and Kiku knocked on the door.

Olivia opened it and blocked the doorway, her smile turning into a frown. "You're back. Without a scratch."

Kiku swallowed her sarcastic reply. "Thank you for watching over him. I have made arrangements for our travel out of Japan with Takeo. As soon as the vet comes back, we will go. Is he awake?"

"He's resting." Olivia crossed her arms.

"If you will excuse me, I wish to speak with Takeo."

Olivia didn't move out of the way. "Daichi was out of this life. You dragged him back in. You need to stay away from him and my sister."

Kiku had already surmised that Olivia was Lilly's sister. She stepped back and held out her hand. "Can we please discuss this out here?"

Olivia stepped into the hallway and pulled the door closed behind her.

Kiku folded her hands in front of herself. "First, do not threaten me. Ever." Olivia opened her mouth to protest, but Kiku's withering gaze cut her off. "Daichi is a man who makes up his own mind. I will let him explain recent developments to you. Until then, know that while I am appreciative of your help, I do not handle threats well. Understood, Doctor?"

Olivia nodded curtly.

"Now, I need to speak with Takeo alone for a moment. Give me five minutes and then be ready to depart."

"He's asleep."

"Waking him now cannot be avoided." Kiku opened the door and slipped into the room.

Takeo was on a cot, fast asleep. His color had returned, and he looked so peaceful, she was hesitant to wake him up. And that wasn't the only reason for her hesitation. The information she was about to give him would change his entire world.

She stroked the back of his arm.

Takeo's eyelids fluttered open. His brown eyes were sharp and clear. A smile spread across his handsome face. "I was wondering where you had gone," he said softly.

"How are you feeling?"

"Now that you're here? Fabulous."

Kiku rolled her eyes, grabbed a chair, and pulled it beside the cot. "What do you remember from the mall?"

Takeo winced as he pulled himself up to a sitting position. "Nothing. I woke up three days ago thinking I was in a kennel. A woman named Olivia checks on me, as does a vet."

Kiku took a deep breath. "Do you remember when I got you out of Fumeiyo no ie?"

"Of course. I was drunk, but I wasn't that drunk."

She shook her head. "You *were* that drunk. But I neglected to tell you something that happened there. It is the reason you were shot." She explained Kenzo's plan to make his own designer heir, and her role in preserving Takeo's seed for that purpose. "It was only because he had your seed that your father thought you were ... dispensable."

She expected a hundred questions—or at least some blame. Takeo gave her neither. Instead he asked, "Did you rescue Jiro?"

"The meeting with Kenzo was a trap that Jiro set. He hoped that Kenzo would kill you and that I would kill him. And just in case those things did not happen, Jiro had the meeting take place next door to the police station, so whoever survived would be arrested. It was a brilliant deception."

Takeo was remarkably calm for someone who'd just found out that both his brother and father wanted him dead. Except that Kenzo wasn't his real father—a fact Kiku dreaded telling him.

"Was Jimmy in on it?"

"He was deceived. Trust me, I interrogated him thoroughly. He is very apologetic."

"He is still alive?" Takeo asked, surprised.

Kiku nodded.

"I need to get back ... what you took from me."

"We recovered it from the fertility clinic where it had been sent. Jimmy, myself, and ..." Kiku cleared her throat. Before she broke the news that Daichi was Takeo's father, she had to tell him that Daichi was alive. "And an old friend," she finished awkwardly.

"Stop. You can't be serious. Did you call him?"

Kiku raised a puzzled eyebrow. There was no way Takeo could know about Daichi's involvement.

"You did." Takeo crossed his arms. "You called Jack Stratton."

"What? Are you seriously letting jealousy—"

"I'm not jealous." From the way Takeo's face scrunched up, she knew he was struggling to decide what to say next. "Stratton is a police officer, and to involve him in ... I mean, he *was* a police officer, but that's still no reason ... Did he come all the way to Japan to help you?"

"Jack did not help me. Your—" Kiku stopped herself. "Daichi helped me. He is alive."

"But ... you killed him years ago."

Kiku folded her hands on her lap and crossed her legs. "No. I was *supposed* to kill him." She watched a flurry of emotions cross Takeo's face—shock, hurt, anger, and finally confusion. "Why wouldn't you tell me? And—why did you let him live?"

"Daichi just wanted out of the Yakuza. He would never betray the organization. He wanted to stop killing, but Kenzo wouldn't let him walk away."

"You brought back his hand."

"He still complains about that often."

Takeo's chuckle grew into a full-blown laugh. After a moment, he winced and held his stomach. "Oh, I'm going to pay for that later, but I needed it. Sorry, I just ... I can picture Uncle Daichi giving you an earful. I can't believe he's alive. And that he's been helping you."

Kiku nodded. "Please do not be upset."

A knock sounded on the door, and Shigeru poked his head in. "Oh, good, you're awake. May I come in?"

Kiku was going to ask for another few minutes alone, but Takeo nodded and Shigeru entered, followed by Olivia.

"How are you feeling?" Shigeru asked.

"Much better, thank you," Takeo said.

"Excellent. You will be traveling soon." Shigeru smiled at Kiku, and the hairs on the back of her neck rose.

She was in close proximity to the man referred to as Death, but that wasn't the reason for her sudden unease; it was because his eyes had changed. Before, there had been a kindness there, a warmth. That was gone now. Even when he smiled, his eyes remained cold.

"Did you secure a ride to the airport?" she asked calmly.

"I have a friend who owns a limo company," Shigeru replied. "He will be here shortly."

"That is wonderful news." Kiku stood, making sure not to seem hurried or uncomfortable. "We will need to get Takeo ready to move." As she twisted slightly toward Takeo, she noted Shigeru's eyes darting to her back, scanning for weapons. It was possible that was merely an old habit. After all, Shigeru had saved Takeo's life, and he was Daichi's friend.

But her gut told her otherwise. She met and held Shigeru's stare. "Twenty million is a lot of money."

His smile did nothing to reassure her. "I will be able to retire."

Takeo sat up straighter, while Olivia slowly stepped toward him and away from Shigeru.

"I do not want to kill you, Shigeru. Daichi is our friend. We will pay you for your help."

"Not twenty million."

Shigeru's eyes became brighter as they talked. His adrenaline must be kicking in. Daichi had always said that Shigeru liked killing.

"You have to be breathing to collect that money," Kiku said. "You know, Daichi told me you're almost as good as he is. And between you and me, I believe him. But I am even better than Daichi."

Shigeru scoffed. "In his day, Daichi was brutally terrifying. But me? They called me Death for a reason. If I had been an artist, they would have called me a master. I have heard of you, Kiku. I listened to all the stories of the girl who should be feared. The demon in the dark. But you are no master."

Kiku nodded. "That is true. I am not a master; I am a monster." Her right hand closed around the grip of her gun.

With incredible speed, Shigeru's scarred right hand seized her right forearm and twisted, sending her gun tumbling from her fingers. That new, cold smile didn't leave his face.

Kiku drew a knife with her left hand and slashed at his carotid artery. Shigeru saw the blade coming and dodged. Yet when his hand went automatically to his throat, blood seeped through his fingers. Kiku had missed the artery, but the wound was deep.

Shigeru whistled, and the door behind him flew open. His son, Touma, stood outside, lowering a shotgun.

Bringing her left arm back across her body, Kiku flung the knife at Touma. The blade turned over once before sticking in the young man's chest.

It wasn't a fatal wound; the lightweight blade penetrated only an inch or two—but it was shocking enough to make him loosen his grip on the shotgun, which clattered to the floor.

Kiku lunged toward Touma, switching her weight to her left leg and kicking with her right. Her heel struck the blade in his chest like a sledgehammer hitting a railroad spike. Touma flew across the hallway, slammed into the wall, and slumped to the floor, unconscious.

Shigeru let out a bellow and punched Kiku hard in the back of her head, sending her stumbling toward Touma's body. Grabbing her hair, he slammed her into the same wall his son had just struck.

Kiku kicked low at Shigeru's knee.

He quickly hopped out of the way, but was forced to release his hold on her.

The door of Takeo's room slammed shut. Olivia had locked herself inside with Takeo. Smart move, under the circumstances, and Kiku was grateful for her instinct to protect Takeo, but Olivia wouldn't be able to save Takeo if Kiku didn't survive this battle.

Kiku and Shigeru eyed each other, circling like sharks, as footsteps rang in the hallway. The dogs in the kennels were going crazy, barking nonstop, and the footsteps belonged to Shigeru's daughters, who took up fighting stances.

Sara moved first, with a flurry of front kicks apparently intended to drive Kiku back toward Shigeru. Kiku grabbed Sara's foot and pinned it against her own hip as she struck Sara in the face with a right cross. Then she pivoted around and flung Sara toward Shigeru. He calmly stepped to the side and let his daughter sail past him and crash to the floor.

Niko brandished a nasty curved knife. Kiku just barely managed to step out of its way and the blade came within millimeters of her stomach. While Kiku tried to keep one eye on Niko and still keep tabs on the other two, Niko swung again and again, advancing with quick, twisting strikes.

Kiku dodged them, but Niko successfully drove her within striking distance of Shigeru, and he punched hard, his left fist catching Kiku in her side just below her ribs. Then a right jab caught her on the chin and sent her stumbling toward Niko.

Too eager for the kill, Niko thrust with her blade. Kiku grabbed Niko's outstretched arm at the wrist, shimmied under her arm, and jacked the girl up by her own arm until the elbow joint snapped.

Kiku flung the screaming girl toward her father. With one powerful arm, he grabbed his daughter by the waist and used her like a battering ram, slamming her legs into Kiku. His fist came around and struck Kiku in the face—one, two, three vicious blows.

The German shepherds were going ballistic, scratching against the window and biting the air. Touma was still out cold, but Sara was back on her feet and returned to the fray.

Kiku kicked low, catching Shigeru's kneecap and driving it backward. As Shigeru roared with pain and stumbled, Sara took his place and began swinging at Kiku. She lacked her father's strength but compensated with speed. A whirlwind of punches and kicks came at Kiku, and a few found their mark. Kiku stepped in, swinging her elbow out in a tight arc. She caught Sara in the jaw and knocked her back into the wall.

Kiku fought to catch her breath. She was fighting a losing battle. Despite all her efforts, she was still trapped between Shigeru and his daughters.

She needed help. And it was readily at hand.

She grabbed the handle of the door to the room holding the German shepherds. The door opened into the hallway, toward her, creating a barrier between her and the dogs. They ran out into the hallway, and there was only one way to go: toward Shigeru's daughters. Niko and Sara shrieked in horror and took off with the dogs chasing after them, and Kiku turned to face Shigeru.

He was looking down at his son. Touma lay on his back, Kiku's knife sticking out of his chest. To Kiku's surprise, he was still breathing.

Shigeru reached for the knife.

"Stop, Shigeru," Kiku said. "Your son is alive. If you take that knife out, he'll bleed to death."

Shigeru's eyes were bright and large. He ripped the knife out of his son's chest and leveled it at Kiku. "I have another son."

Kiku flexed her hands. "I will kill you now."

Shigeru laughed as he spun the knife in his fingers. "Do you know who I am? I. AM. *DEATH!*"

A deafening shotgun blast stopped his speech, punching a hole through the quarantine room door and striking Shigeru full-on.

The quarantine room door swung open, pushing aside Shigeru's lifeless body, and Takeo leaned against the doorframe, a smoking shotgun in his hands. "You really have to explain to me what the hell is going on."

"I will tell you everything on the plane." Kiku gently put her arm around his waist. "Can you walk?"

Takeo nodded. "Slowly."

"Fine. Give me the shotgun." Kiku looked into the room. "Are you coming, Olivia?"

Olivia stared at the bodies on the floor. Wide-eyed, she nodded.

"Where are we going?" Takeo asked.

"America."

26

On the plane ride, Kiku had filled Takeo in on everything that had transpired. Everything except who his real father was. She felt it wasn't her place to share that information, even though Daichi wanted Takeo to know.

But now, as they drove out to Daichi's farm—Kiku driving, Takeo in the passenger seat, Olivia sleeping in the back—she wondered if that had been a horrible mistake. How would Takeo react when he discovered that she'd kept this from him? Even if she'd done so only for a short time.

"What are you thinking about?" Takeo asked.

"Daichi," Kiku admitted.

"Did he take the news about Shigeru hard?"

Kiku scowled. "No. He said, 'I guess a leopard can't change its spots. That guy always was evil.' In fact, he tried to twist it around like I should have known. It is ridiculous. He is ridiculous. He was Shigeru's partner."

"Do you know when you two argue it sounds like a father-daughter thing?"

Kiku shuddered. "Do not say that."

Takeo shrugged. "I don't mean for it to sound creepy." He started to reach for his water bottle, winced, and leaned back again.

"You have pushed yourself too hard," Kiku admonished. She grabbed the water bottle from the cup holder and unscrewed the cap for him. "We should have taken another day at the hotel. When we get to the farm, you are going to bed immediately."

"Is that an offer?"

Kiku blushed and glanced quickly at the back seat, but Olivia was still asleep. "I am serious. Olivia agrees. You almost died."

"No." Takeo shook his head. "I was almost *murdered*. And while my father hunts us down, I run off into the desert to hide like a prairie dog."

"It will not be for long."

"You said Daichi's legs were broken and the doctors think it will be months before he recovers." Takeo tapped his knuckle against the window. "And Olivia believes it will be at least two months until I am able to exert myself—though I know she is wrong."

"We will discuss Kenzo later. I am working on a plan. You need to speak with Daichi." Kiku checked her mirrors as she turned onto the dirt road leading up to the farm. She had taken extreme measures to ensure they weren't followed, but her head was still on a swivel. "And Alex."

Though she was uneasy about his conversation with Daichi, she knew that for Takeo, it was speaking to Alex that made him nervous.

The farm had a new gate, and barbed-wire fencing now ran in both directions. As she approached, the gate opened with a metallic click. She noticed the metal plate installed beneath it—most likely complete with tire spikes. *Hwan has been busy.*

When Kiku stopped the car to let the gate open, Olivia sat up in the back seat, rubbing her eyes. She looked around expectantly and frowned when she didn't see a house.

"We are almost there," Kiku said, pulling forward. "Your sister will be happy to see you."

As they continued up to the house, she noticed several cameras and some curiously placed animal feeders. Hwan was taking security very seriously.

They rounded the last turn, and she spotted Alex's black hair peeking from around the barn. She wondered who was most nervous about this get-together: Takeo, Alex, or Daichi.

As she parked, the farmhouse door flew open and Lilly raced down a new accessibility ramp. Olivia bolted out of the car and the sisters embraced for the first time in more than twelve years.

Baba walked out on the porch wiping her hands on her apron, but when Kiku got out of the car, she kept her hand by her thigh and gave Kiku a thumbs-down—the Japanese equivalent of the middle finger.

Hwan pushed Daichi's wheelchair out onto the porch and parked him there. Daichi met Kiku's eye, and from his intense stare, she knew he was wondering if she had told Takeo that he was his father.

Kiku shook her head, and Daichi scowled. Kiku studied him for a brief moment and determined that except for his annoyance with her, he was glad to be home and healing well. There would be time enough for explanations, reunions, and confessing of secrets. She only cared that she had gotten Takeo here safely.

She opened Takeo's door and helped him out of the car. Lilly and Olivia hurried over to assist. Daichi's wife took one look at Takeo and gasped.

"I'm sorry. I'm Lilly." She carefully wrapped her arms around his shoulders and gave him a hug, her tears running freely.

Takeo cast a desperate look at Kiku as Lilly pressed her damp cheek against his face.

Kiku shrugged and smiled at him. *What does he want me to do? Shoot the woman?*

"Let's get you inside," Lilly said. She took one of Takeo's arms, Olivia the other, and they helped him inside like they were escorting an old man into a nursing home. To Kiku's surprise, Takeo not only didn't insist on getting into the house under his own power, but he seemed to enjoy being pampered.

Baby.

Baba went back inside as well, with a scowl for Kiku.

Kiku looked around for Alex, but the boy remained out of sight.

"Takeo needs to rest," Kiku said, as his two blond nurses walked him into the house. Takeo cast an annoyed look at her over his shoulder.

"We'll get him right as soon as we can," Lilly cooed. She rubbed Takeo's back and spoke in a mothering tone. "We've set up a room for you on the first floor so you don't have to worry about the stairs, but it's not quite ready. For now, we'll get you settled in the living room."

Kiku turned to Hwan and Daichi.

"I see you have been upgrading security on the farm." She pulled several candy bars from her purse, her usual bribe for Hwan.

Hwan's face lit up, and he bowed as he took the gift. "I can't wait to show you. Alex and I have been busy."

"Busy." Daichi shook his head. "They've installed turrets. I'm not kidding."

"I did not think you were. Nor would I have expected less." Kiku winked at Hwan, and his large chest puffed up. "I would love a tour, but I need to speak to Daichi first. Privately. And where is Alex?"

"I'll go find him," Hwan said cheerily through a mouthful of Belgian milk chocolate.

"How is Jimmy?" Kiku asked Daichi.

"Fine. Sleeping, his second-favorite activity." Daichi wheeled closer to Kiku. "Between him, Hwan, and Alex, my grocery bill has gone up to ten times what it was. Those three never stop eating, and Baba is cooking sunup to sundown."

"She probably loves it, and you have plenty of money. That is not why you are upset."

"You didn't tell Takeo. You said you would."

"I changed my mind. It is not my place. That responsibility is—"

"He's my WHAT?" Takeo roared from the living room.

"Uh-oh ..." Daichi closed his eyes and let his head roll forward onto his chest, as if preparing to meet a tidal wave head-on.

Kiku strode into the house and ran into Lilly, Olivia, and Baba beating a hasty retreat from the room where Takeo was bellowing, "Kiku!"

Lilly looked at Kiku apologetically. "Daichi said you were going to tell him," she whispered.

Kiku patted her arm. "I wish I had. But I will deal with it now."

She found Takeo standing alone in the middle of the living room, chin raised, shoulders back, feet apart. "You *knew*?" he said through clenched teeth.

"I found out in Noshiro."

Takeo's nostrils flared. "You and I are supposed to have no secrets. I have kept none from you."

"I have kept several from you. For that, I apologize." Kiku bowed low. "I felt it was not my place to tell you."

She straightened to attention and rested her gaze on his neck, not looking into his eyes directly, as a sign of respect. He crossed his arms—his signal that their conversation was over.

The blurred lines of their relationship had never been more clear than in this moment. "I apologize for speaking," Kiku said in a soothing tone and with another bow, in the role of his employee. Then she raised her head and continued in a strong voice, as his lover. "To you, heritage is everything. I have lived my life knowing that with my ancestry, I am considered a dog. I have never been jealous of your bloodline. I shared your pride in it. In some ways, I mourn that you have lost that. Although I cannot fully know your pain, if you allow, I can bear some of it."

She bowed low, then stepped to the side when she heard the whir of Daichi's wheelchair motor. Daichi stopped in front of Takeo, and the two men stared at one another. As Kiku looked on, she felt foolish she hadn't made the connection before. Here, side by side, there was no denying their likeness. Kiku wondered who would speak first.

Daichi removed the blanket from across his waist and held up two brown bottles. "You want to grab a beer and go talk outside?"

Takeo nodded and took the bottles, while Kiku stood there like a koi, her mouth open, no sound coming out. The men were on their way out when Alex ran into the room and straight to Daichi, while Takeo stopped in his tracks.

"You're my *grandfather*? Seriously? All this time I've been here and you don't tell me you're my *grandfather*?" He grabbed both handles of the wheelchair and got right in Daichi's face.

Daichi smiled. "Surprise."

Alex pressed his palms against the sides of his head like he was trying to keep it from exploding. "What is *wrong* with this family?!" He turned and glared at Takeo.

Takeo frowned. "I didn't even know you existed. When I found out, I—"

"Sent Kiku to get me," Alex snapped. "You didn't even come yourself." He stepped forward, and so did Takeo.

"I didn't know if your mother was telling the truth," Takeo said. "I needed to be certain you were ..." His voice trailed off.

"I was what?" Alex thrust his chin out.

"My son." Takeo bowed low. "Forgive me."

Kiku's eyes widened as Takeo held his bow.

Alex looked at Kiku with confusion. She turned her palm over and opened and closed her fingers rapidly as she bowed ever so slightly.

"Bow back to him," Daichi whispered, too loudly.

Alex bowed awkwardly, then father and son straightened up and stared at each other.

Daichi wheeled around and pushed Alex's butt with his foot. "Give him a hug, doofus."

Kiku expected Alex to protest, but the teenager burst into tears and threw his arms around Takeo. As his body rocked with his sobs, Takeo held him and patted his back.

Kiku started to slip out of the room, but Daichi grabbed her hand. She leaned close to him and he whispered, "You better grab another beer."

She narrowed her eyes. "Alex is only thirteen."

Daichi made a face. "I, ah ... meant for me."

Kiku smiled. "Go talk to your son. You will be fine. There is something I need to do."

27

Kiku poured herself a cup of tea, while Baba chopped onions at the kitchen table.

"Will you be staying long enough to finish the job?" Baba asked.

Kiku raised a puzzled eyebrow. She was confused not only by the question but by the very fact that Baba was speaking to her.

"Excuse me?"

"Daichi, Jimmy, and Takeo are still alive," Baba said, "and it looks like you want to get them all killed. So, will you stick around only until they're dead, or will you be staying until you get Hwan and Alex killed, too?"

Kiku sat down at the table. The old woman chopped with gusto, no doubt expecting Kiku to flee the uncomfortable situation. But Kiku never retreated.

"I am trying to save their lives."

"Ha!" Baba picked up the cutting board, dumped the onions in a pot, and set it down loudly. "Then why don't you go to the police?"

Now it was Kiku's turn to laugh. "*That* we cannot do."

"See?" Baba pointed her knife at Kiku as she picked up some carrots. "Instead, you drag Daichi back into the Yakuza."

"Takeo is trying to change the Yakuza. He wants to make it legitimate."

"But Daichi was out."

"You are never out."

"That's a lie." Baba sliced the carrots into thin disks, her knife flying across the cutting board. "You don't have to be Yakuza."

"I had no choice."

"When you were a child, you did not." Baba stopped chopping and looked Kiku in the eye. "But you aren't a child anymore. You can leave."

"I stay for other reasons."

"Money." Baba turned her head and pretended to spit on the floor. "The root of all evil."

"You are wrong about me and money." Kiku sipped her tea. "As I said, I have other reasons for remaining in the Yakuza, but those reasons are my own. Secondly, the Apostle Paul said it was the *love* of money that is the root of all evil. Money is an object. In and of itself it is neutral. But when someone evil, like Kenzo, loves money ..." Kiku trailed off as an idea flickered to life in the back of her mind.

Baba slammed her knife down on the board. "Go on."

Kiku's eyes widened. "We *can* go to the police." She jumped up, seized Baba's shoulders, and shouted, "You are brilliant!"

"Of course I am." Baba pushed Kiku away. "Keep your hands off me. Where are you going?"

"If you will excuse me," Kiku said, running out of the kitchen, "I must speak with Jimmy."

She found Jimmy lying in bed watching TV in his room upstairs, both of his arms in slings. She turned off the TV and stood at his bedside.

He sat up as straight as he could given the bandages, eyes wide. "What's going on? Did Kenzo find the farm?"

"No. I need to find Jiro."

Jimmy exhaled. "You totally freaked me out running in here like that." He leaned back onto his pillows. "I thought Kenzo was at the gate."

"He will be, unless we stop him. That is why I need to find Jiro."

"I don't know where he is."

"But you hung out together. You were his friend."

"He could be anywhere on the planet. We hung out in Hong Kong, but Jiro also liked to go to Miami, New York, Ibiza ... Like I said, he could be anywhere."

"Jiro is a serial dater. Does he have a current girlfriend?"

"Girlfriend? Is that what we're calling them?" Jimmy rolled his eyes. "The last one was a stripper we met in a club. I think her name was Linda. I can never keep them straight. I guess they 'dated.'" He made air quotes. "Jiro bought a lot of crap for her. He's a nerd, but he sure likes to party."

"If you needed to get Jiro a message, besides using a phone, how did you contact him?"

"Usually, we'd call. Or we'd message each other in *Battle World*."

"Battle what?"

"World," Alex said from the doorway to his room across the hall. "It's a PvP MMO."

Kiku raised an eyebrow. "Can you please translate that?"

"It's a massive multiplayer online game that's mostly player versus player, although you can team up, and even clan together," Alex explained.

"And Jiro contacts you in this video game?" Kiku asked Jimmy.

He nodded. "But he won't anymore, since he knows I'm with you."

"Do you play this game on a computer or one of those boxes?"

"Console," Alex corrected her in a voice only a thirteen-year-old admonishing an adult could pull off. "You can play on either. Why?"

"Will it tell you where Jiro is?"

Alex looked at Jimmy, and they both shrugged.

"I don't think so," Alex said. "But you can tell when someone is online. What's his gamertag?" he asked Jimmy.

"Lady Killa," Jimmy said. "Capital L, capital K. But with fours for 'a' and an exclamation point for the 'i.'"

Alex laughed. "What a dork. How old is he?"

"Twenty-eight, but he still behaves like a child," Kiku said. She pulled out her phone. "I have a friend who will know if we can use this gamertag to track Jiro. Alex, can you first check if he is currently logged in?"

"Hwan set me up with a great computer," Alex bragged. "Come on up to my room."

Kiku turned Jimmy's TV back on and followed Alex to his room.

Alex's room had a single bed, a wall-mounted TV, and a corner desk with a computer on it. The place was immaculate.

The boy smiled nervously as he sat at the desk. "Do you like my room?"

"It is wonderful. You seem happy here."

"I am." Alex booted up his computer. "I never had a room before. My own, I mean. It was always a room with, like, six other kids. They've been really nice to me here. All of them."

"Even Daichi?" Kiku joked.

"Did you know?" Alex didn't look at her.

She shook her head. "I just found out."

"He's a good guy."

Kiku nodded. Daichi *was* a "good guy"—no matter what Daichi himself believed.

Alex started up *Battle World*.

"Will Jiro know you are looking him up in the game?" Kiku asked.

"No." He pulled up a box and typed in the gamertag, and a green light appeared next to the name. "He's online. Do you want me to send him a friend request?"

"No. Hold on." She dialed a number on her phone.

"Who are you calling?"

"A friend. She's a computer expert."

The phone rang three times before Alice answered.

"Hey, Kiku."

"Good evening, Alice." Kiku put the call on speaker and explained the situation to Alice.

Alice clicked her tongue. "I might be able to tell you something, but I'd need to be on the PC you're using. Can I remote in?"

"Sure," Alex said.

It didn't take long for Alice to establish a remote connection that allowed her to control Alex's computer. Two windows opened on the screen: one contained strings of text, and the other was a video feed of Alice.

"Nice to meet you, Alex," Alice said, smiling. "Any friend of Kiku's is a friend of mine. Kiku, you look great, as always."

Alex placed a hand over his camera and mouthed to Kiku, *She's smoking hot.*

Kiku smacked the back of his head. "Do you think you will be able to assist us, Alice?"

"Yes, but Alex was right. There's not much I can tell you without friending Jiro. I searched the internet, but his gamertag isn't linked to any social media accounts."

"I can friend him," Alex offered. "Or I can send him a game invite."

Kiku placed a hand on his shoulder. "Wait. How do you invite him? Is it text, or can you use video?"

"Either one," Alex answered.

"Alice, since you can control Alex's computer, can you invite Jiro to the game?"

Alice made a face. "I don't know how to play."

Alex's chest puffed up. "I do. I'm awesome. I can invite him."

"No." Kiku lightly squeezed his shoulder. "Alice, would it be possible for Alex to play the game and for you to send the video message?"

Alice's nose wrinkled. "Sure, but why?"

"I think it would be better bait if the invitation comes from someone who is ..." Kiku looked down at Alex. "How did you say it, Alex? Smoking hot?"

Alex blushed and tried to lean out of view of the camera, but Kiku held him in place. Alice was blushing, too.

"Before we start," Kiku said, "I have to tell you there is a risk, Alice. Jiro is a dangerous man, and this will allow him to see your face."

Alice's reaction was excitement, not fear. "I love going undercover. I'm in."

"Good. Then shift your camera so we only see your face and the wall behind you. And please do not let Lady into the shot. The less he knows about you, the better." Kiku inhaled slowly. "Is Jack home?"

"No, he's out." Alice smiled impishly. "We're good. I can cover my tracks. Should I try to look younger?" She started pulling her hair into a ponytail.

Kiku smiled. "You're only twenty-one."

Alex sat up straighter in his chair. "Really?" His voice rose.

"Alice is marrying a former police officer next month," Kiku said sternly. "A very *overprotective* former police officer."

Alice zoomed her camera in so it only captured her shoulders and face. "Okay, I think this is good. Alex, all you'll have to do is play the game. I'll stay on video, pretending like I'm playing it, but really I'll be trying to scrape Jiro's location info from the server."

Alex nodded. "Okay."

Alice closed her eyes, bowed her head for a moment, then nodded and grinned. "Showtime!"

Kiku shook her head. She didn't know who was a bigger adrenaline junkie, Alice or Jack.

Alice recorded a message—"Hey, Lady Killa! You up for getting your butt kicked in a game?"—and sent it. Then she looked into the camera. "Okay, guys, I'm muting you so he won't be able to hear you, but I can still see you. Wave if you need me."

A window with Jiro's face popped up almost immediately. "Hi!" He was sitting in a high-back chair with a headset on. "Yeah. Sure." He pushed his glasses up his nose. "I'll try to go easy on you."

Alex flexed his fingers and grabbed his mouse. While Alex played, Alice did an exceptional job of pantomiming. Of course, since the camera was focused on her from the shoulders up, that wasn't very difficult.

When Jiro won, Alex swore, Alice scowled, and Jiro preened.

"Who kicked whose butt?" Jiro swiveled back and forth in his chair. Each time he turned, Kiku caught a slight view of the window behind him. The Eiffel Tower was visible in the distance.

Paris? Except it didn't look like Paris.

She took out her phone and texted Alice. *Can you take a picture of his screen? I can see outside.*

Alice texted back a thumbs-up, followed by, *Got his IP.*

"What is an IP?" Kiku asked Alex.

"It's the address of his computer. It means she's working on finding out where he is. But, um ... I kinda need to concentrate if you want me to beat him."

Kiku rolled her eyes. She did not care in the slightest who won this video game.

They played for almost two hours, and Alice and Jiro chatted away through most of it. Alex's and Jiro's skill levels were close, but Alex ended up with the most wins, and clearly this was a point of pride for the young man.

Kiku focused on the window behind Jiro. Only occasionally did she catch a glimpse of it as he rotated in his chair, and only a sliver. After a while, she started recording the computer monitor with her phone.

Finally, Alice texted. *Got his location. Keep going?*

Wrap it up, Kiku texted back.

At the end of the next game, Alice stretched. "Well, it's been fun, but I gotta work in the morning."

"Yeah. Me too," Jiro said. "Are you going to be online tomorrow?"

"Could be." Alice shrugged. "I'll message you for a game if I am."

"Deal." Jiro smiled.

All sympathy Kiku had ever had for the shy man was gone. She wanted more than anything to reach through the PC and shoot the goofy grin off his face.

After terminating the connection, Alice unmuted Alex's mic and spun around in her chair. "Woot! That was sweet!" She pounded out a quick drum solo on her desk. "Way to go, Alex!"

"I let him win a couple of matches to make it look good," Alex boasted.

Kiku patted his shoulder. "You did well, Alex."

"You did awesome!" Alice gave him a big thumbs-up, and Alex blushed again. "And I think *I* did a pretty good job of going undercover."

"You were great!" Alex gushed. "It looked like you were really playing."

Cutting through the congratulations, Kiku asked, "What is his location?"

"Las Vegas. The Sun Garden Resort."

"Not Paris? I saw the Eiffel Tower," Alex said.

"That's not the real one—just a Vegas replica. Vegas is crazy," Alice said.

"Can you tell the floor or room?" Kiku asked.

Alice shook her head. "The IP is forward-facing so I can only tell the building. See, all the IPs in the building go through their hardware, and only the building's IP is seen by the internet. But I did take some screenshots of his window, like you asked. Hang on."

A screenshot of Jiro and his hotel room filled Alex's monitor. The replica Eiffel Tower was visible out the window.

"I've got some programs that should be able to compute the floor using this image," Alice said. "And I might even be able to get the room."

"That would be perfect. How long will it take you?"

"How long do I have?" Alice shot back, ready for the challenge.

"I will be in Las Vegas in five hours."

28

The testosterone in the living room was overwhelming after Kiku briefed Takeo and Daichi.

"No," Takeo said.

Daichi nodded. "I agree with Takeo. We should wait."

"You are mistaken if you think I was asking for permission. I was simply informing you of my decision."

Takeo bristled, but Daichi wisely cut him off before he erupted. "Your plan is brilliant. Jiro knows where all of Kenzo's financial skeletons are buried. But he'll never testify against Kenzo."

"He will now. And that is why I have to leave immediately. I am surprised that Jiro is still alive. I would have thought that Kenzo would have already annihilated him for his betrayal and besmirching the Nakumora name."

Takeo was pacing the room between Daichi's wheelchair and Kiku, who stood firm with her arms crossed. "It's too dangerous. Jiro tried to kill us. Let Kenzo take him out. It is what my brother deserves."

"Once Kenzo is finished with Jiro, he *will* come for us, Takeo. We must take Kenzo down, and this is the only way to do that. You both know it is true."

"You can't do it on your own," Takeo said.

"I will take Hwan."

Kiku got in the driver's seat, and Hwan took the passenger seat. As they drove away, Daichi started yelling.

"What's he yelling about?" Hwan asked.

Kiku held up Daichi's pack of cigarettes. "He needs to quit."

Hwan's laughter trailed off as Kiku turned off the driveway and headed for the barn. "Did you forget something?"

"Someone plans to follow us."

Hwan sat bolt upright.

"Stay in the car. I will deal with this."

Kiku got out of the car and walked quietly to the barn. She opened the smaller door. "Alex, what are you doing?"

Alex was frozen in the act of putting a bag in the motorcycle saddle. "I ... I wasn't ..." He took a deep breath and straightened up. "I can shoot. Daichi taught me. A pistol and a rifle."

"You are not in the plan. I need you here. You and Alice are the keys to luring Jiro out."

"Jimmy can do it. He can kinda move his arms now."

"No. For many reasons. Most importantly, I do not want blood on your hands. You must take care of your life. And this life"—she touched her chest—"is not yours."

"It's my heritage." Alex lifted his chin and pulled back his shoulders.

Kiku wanted to slap him. "You sound like Kenzo. Let me tell you a secret: a great man looks within. Your father could be a king, but if you turned into a scumbag, you would just be the scumbag son of a king." She grabbed Alex's chin, held it fast, and looked into his eyes. "You, Alex Nakumora, will be a great man."

Alex frowned. "A great man playing a video game?"

"You are performing your part, and it is an important one. If you fail, Jiro will get away, Kenzo will win, and we will all die."

Alex's eyes glistened—whether from excitement or fear, Kiku wasn't sure. Perhaps it was a combination of the two ... if so, Alex had the makings of a fine warrior.

Kiku smiled and headed for the door. "If it is honor you want, stay here and stick to the plan." She stopped with her hand on the worn iron handle. "If I fail, and Kenzo comes here ... then, and only then, will you fight."

Alex nodded, his face solemn.

As Kiku returned to the car, she watched two horses cantering and swishing their tails in a nearby field. Kiku would have given anything to grow up here. This farm was a good place. Alex could grow into a good man here—and Daichi could age into a happy old one.

She would not fail. She couldn't.

But as she watched the horses gallop over a hill, she wondered if she would ever see any of this again, and whether Alex would live to be the man she knew he could be.

29

After a short flight in the private plane arranged by Daichi, Kiku and Hwan hopped in the BMW that Daichi had waiting for them, and drove to a mini-mart. Kiku slipped into the women's restroom to change into a clingy, low-cut dress and apply full-glam, night-on-the-town makeup. She emerged, winked at the love-smitten attendants as she walked by the counter, and waited for Hwan by the car.

When Hwan reappeared, he looked nothing like his affable old self. He'd shaved off his beard and had traded in his retro T-shirt for a three-piece suit.

"How do I look?"

"Too good." Kiku grinned as she loosened his tie and unbuttoned the top button of his shirt. "Drink this." She handed him a Jack Daniel's nip.

Hwan downed the whiskey in one gulp and licked his lips. Kiku opened another nip and poured some into the palm of her hand, then dipped her fingertips into the puddle of liquor and flicked the alcohol into Hwan's face.

"Ow! Ow!" Hwan rubbed his eyes. "Are you trying to blind me?"

"Do not take it personally," Kiku said as she spritzed the booze onto her own face. "We are playing a part. Let me do the talking, however. Just look stern."

"Stern?" Hwan blinked rapidly, his eyes bloodshot. "Can I look nervous as hell? Because that's what I am."

"No. You need to act cool or we will get killed."

Hwan shook his head. "That's not helping."

"You will be fine. Just follow my lead. You need to drive."

"But now I smell like booze."

"The police are the least of our worries. It is only two blocks. We need to drop the bag off first."

They got into their car, and Hwan started it up. "Run it through for me again."

Kiku repeated the intel she'd gotten from Alice. "Jiro is on the twenty-eighth floor, room two-eight-seven-seven—the penthouse normally reserved for high rollers. It isn't actually on the top floor, but they call it the penthouse, for sex appeal. Above it are two floors of office space and conference rooms."

Hwan turned down a side street and pulled up at the end of an alley, where Kiku handed him the trash bag and a tire iron. Hwan ran twenty feet down the alley, tossed the bag next to a dumpster, set the tire iron down next to it, and jogged back.

They drove back onto the brightly lit streets of Las Vegas. Neon blinked and flashed from every corner. Scantily clad tourists paraded by, while music wafted from all the grand hotels. The decision to arrive in Vegas a bit later than originally planned was a good one. Kiku didn't want to be there too far in advance of taking action.

Soon they approached the Sun Garden Resort, owned and operated by the Yakuza. Though it boasted its share of glitz and lights, the Sun Garden was more tasteful and sleeker than its neighbors, with a modern Asian design.

"You know what to do," Kiku said.

Hwan cleared his throat and cracked his neck to loosen up. He pulled up to the valet station, popped the trunk open, and said in his best imitation of a stern, manly voice, "Room fourteen-oh-two," dangling the keys nonchalantly as he got out of the car.

Kiku stumbled out on her side, giggling. "Just like the poem." Everyone looked puzzled, and she recited like a schoolgirl, "In four-

a king-size bed near the window, Kiku and Hwan immediately swept for bugs and hidden cameras, and found several of each. Kiku changed the angles on the cameras so they wouldn't see anything useful and left one bug in the closet, in front of the radio, which she tuned to annoying pop music. They got to work unpacking the weapons and tactical gear, including a tandem BASE-jumping parachute.

"Can you believe Daichi took Lilly BASE jumping?" she said.

"Is that what he told you?" Hwan laughed. "It's the other way around—Lilly had skydived before and loved it. She thought Daichi would enjoy the thrill, so she surprised him one birthday. It turned out it wasn't a good surprise. Daichi hates heights."

Kiku smiled as she recalled how well he'd hidden his fear during their rock-climbing race. Quickly, another image appeared in her mind: Daichi plummeting down the side of the building, then his twisted legs after the fall.

If he hated heights so much, why didn't he say anything? Especially after the rock climbing? Her heart told her the answer: it was so Kiku wouldn't have to go alone.

"What do I do now?" Hwan asked.

"Are you dressed underneath?" Kiku reached her hand into his shirt, and Hwan blushed and skittered away.

"Yeah, I'm wearing it underneath the suit. That's why I look so big." Hwan's smile dimmed.

"That Australian man outside the elevator is the leader of Kenzo's B-Team security. His name is Nelson, and he is a mean fool. You kept your cover well."

"That didn't bother me," Hwan said. From the way his eyes flitted around, it was clear to her he was lying.

"Nor should it. You are big-boned. And very strong." Kiku winked and got a small smile out of him. "Now, you need to get your gear together while Alice gets to work."

Hwan patted his jacket. "I have everything I need."

Kiku checked her watch. "It will be light soon. You should get going." She handed Hwan a hotel key. "Stay safe."

"You too." He headed out the door.

Kiku pulled out her laptop and phone and called Alice. "Hello, Alice," Kiku said. "The laptop is on."

Alice replied to Kiku's cut-to-the-chase, all-business start with a bit of sarcasm. "'Hi, Alice. How are you?' 'Hey, Kiku. I'm fine. Glad you got there safe and sound,'" she quipped.

"Forgive me. I am on the job and I forgot how sensitive you are."

"Touché." Alice laughed. "I get it. Jack's manners go out the window when he is on task."

"Excuse me, but we must work quickly, Alice."

"Right! So, don't log in to the hotel Wi-Fi. Can you connect through your phone hotspot? I'll tunnel in."

Kiku wasn't the most experienced expert with devices, but she managed to complete Alice's request. "I speak a number of languages, but I wish I could speak tech as well as you."

"Remember, we said you wouldn't have to worry about this part." Alice typed away. "I'm connected to your laptop. Just need a minute." Windows began popping up all over Kiku's screen, including the hotel's Wi-Fi login prompt. "I'm installing a password grabber program. It'll screw up your laptop so you won't be able to connect to the hotel's Wi-Fi. You'll call for technical support, and when they can't fix it—and trust me, they won't be able to—have them send someone up to the room. They won't be able to get your laptop to connect to the Wi-Fi either, so they'll log in through the administrator console and we'll grab their password. Then we can log in as an administrator, and I should be able to access everything. You got all that?"

"I understand enough. Thank you, Alice."

"Easy-peasy. Call me once they've finished with your laptop."

Kiku hung up. She very much hoped this would work. She not only had to get Jiro off the twenty-eighth floor, but she would then have to make it two floors up to the roof, all without running into hotel security or Kenzo's detail, both headed by Nelson.

And if Alice couldn't get access to the video feed, Kiku would have to go in blind.

30

Hwan stepped out of the hotel's quiet, cool ambience into the neon glow of Las Vegas. The desert sky was already starting to lighten and he had a lot to do. He tried to act calm as he approached the alley where they had stopped earlier, but sweat poured down his face and his shirt clung to his back.

The truth was, he wasn't made for this. Hwan had been only thirteen when he joined the Yakuza—and it hadn't been by choice. He'd come from a well-to-do family and had a pampered life—but he was also a chubby kid and was constantly picked on. The older he got, the bigger he grew. In middle school, the teasing turned to taunting, and the threats turned to action.

One day, on the way home from school, he got jumped by six boys with sticks. He could still hear the ringleader yelling, "Hit the piñata until the candy comes out!" He'd been messed with before—spat on, punched, generally humiliated—but these kids really wanted to hurt him. He was scared.

And then two older guys showed up, out of the blue, on a motorcycle, and demonstrated that when it came to violence, the boys were amateurs. Hwan didn't see the whole fight, because the tough guys ordered him to go home, but what he did see was shockingly brutal. All the kids ended up in the hospital and were out of school for weeks.

Hwan wasn't bullied after that, and for that he was grateful. But about a month later, his rescuers stopped him on his way home. They explained, in no uncertain terms, that Hwan was now indebted to the Yakuza. And the Yakuza expected debts to be repaid in full.

They started him off with simple jobs, like lookout and courier. In every task he failed spectacularly. When he was a lookout, everything looked like a threat to him—except for the undercover policemen whom he failed to notice. When he was a courier, he was so anxious to rid himself of the drugs strapped to his waist that he once mistakenly delivered them to the wrong address. Even among the Yakuza, he became an outcast among the outcasts.

Until he met Kiku.

Kiku saw his limitations, but she never gave up on him. She kept giving him different tasks until she found something he was good at: building things. And even then, he had setbacks. When he reinforced her Audi with bulletproof glass, he made the glass too thick to slide into the door, and as a result, the window wouldn't go up and down. He expected her to be furious, but that wasn't what happened. She came back, the car riddled with bullet strikes, and praised him, claiming the glass had saved her life. From that day on, he knew he'd do anything for Kiku.

He also knew she had to be in dire straits to be relying on him for this sort of job. Sure, Daichi, Takeo, and Jimmy were all out of commission—but even so, he had to believe she'd rather beg anyone else to help but him. He just hoped he wouldn't let her down.

He stepped behind the dumpster in the alley and pulled off his jacket and shirt. Underneath, he wore an electrical service shirt. *Simple but effective*, Kiku had said. Then he retrieved the trash bag and tire iron from where he'd left them. Using the tire iron, he removed the manhole cover in the middle of the alley. His heart hammered in his chest as he looked down at the small opening.

I can fit, I can fit, he coached himself as he started down the ladder.

His stomach stopped him. He sucked it in and tried to shake himself down. He hooked one foot beneath a ladder rung in order to pull from below. His shirt bunched up around his chest, then his stomach popped through suddenly and he lost his footing. The bag dropped from his hand, but he managed to hook one arm over a rung and stopped himself from falling. Muttering, grumbling, and cursing, he flicked on his flashlight and pulled the manhole cover closed above his head. It slipped into place with a clang, and he tried not to think about being trapped underground. Those days he'd spent stuck in the attic of the safe house after helping Kiku and Alex escape had made him deathly afraid of being imprisoned and alone.

At the bottom of the ladder, he wiped the sweat from his face. He shined the light on the bag and inspected his equipment. The receiver seemed fine, but the circuit board with the mass of wires hanging off it ... he had no idea. He'd cobbled the thing together using information from the dark web and electrical forums, but he wasn't even certain it worked *before* he dropped it. And he wasn't sure how far his remote signal would reach, considering the electrical box was underground.

He grabbed the bag and made his way down the tunnel. Apart from its funky odor, the tunnel wasn't what he'd expected. He thought he'd be wading through water with rats and garbage floating by, but this was more like walking through a narrow, dry basement.

He found the electrical case, picked the lock, and pulled it open. When he'd explained to Kiku how he planned to bring down the system, he'd compared it to trying to pull open a bag of potato chips. You couldn't just pull anywhere on the bag; you had to find that little notched spot. If you tore right there, the bag would open easily. And this electrical case was that little notch. If he tripped the electricity here, he'd bring down the whole bag of chips—the grid that made the glow of Las Vegas visible from outer space. That was the theory, anyway.

He prayed he was right. Because if he was wrong ...

Kiku would soon be dead.

31

Kiku sat impatiently in Room 1402. It was getting close to ten p.m. and Jiro still wasn't online. Hwan had called Kiku seven times since setting up his equipment that morning. He had rented a car and a van, and both vehicles were now in place. Kiku hoped he could keep it together for a few hours more.

Alice's plan to gain access to the hotel's security system had gone perfectly, and now they could both call up video feeds from any camera in the building. Currently, they were watching the camera at the end of the hallway on the twenty-eighth floor. Two men were stationed outside Jiro's door.

"There are an awful lot of guys," Alice said over video chat. "I've counted six men so far."

"I would estimate closer to twice that number," Kiku said.

"A dozen guys? Kiku, this is crazy. How can you possibly hope to get Jiro past that pack of guard dogs?" Alice looked worried. "Don't you think you should go to the police? If you don't want to work with the local cops, Jack is friends with both state and federal—"

"I have a plan."

"It better be one humdinger of a plan. Like the best plan ever. All of those guys are armed."

"It is." The weight of the parachute was heavy on Kiku's shoulders.

She was burning energy by wearing it now, but it was best to have it on in case she had to move in a hurry.

"I have seen that you can control the cameras," Kiku said. "Can you control anything else? What about interior lights?"

"I'm afraid not. They're not connected to the computer systems. And even if I could, they have emergency lighting for when the power goes off."

"But they don't have emergency lights on the roof, correct?"

"Affirmative. If the power goes off when you're up there, it's going to be pitch-black." Alice frowned. "Oh, snap! Jiro just came online."

"I am switching over to my earpiece. Are you ready?"

"We are a go, baby!" Alice tapped her headset. "I have both you and Jiro in my ear, so keep that in mind."

"Test one, two, three. Come in," Kiku said into her microphone.

Hwan answered. "I got you."

"Me too," Alex said. "I thought you guys were never going to be ready. I've been sitting here waiting around—"

"Quiet, Alex," said Kiku. "Are you ready?"

"All set," Alex grumbled.

"Hey, buddy!" Alice quickly added. "Let's kick this guy's butt tonight. I'm good to go."

Kiku picked up her equipment bag and headed to the door. "Alice, once you confirm that Jiro is there, give me the go signal."

"Will do."

Kiku rested the heavy gear bag as she held the door handle. The minutes ticked by slowly. Finally, Jiro joined the online game.

"Hey, you're on late tonight," Alice said.

"I was hoping you were waiting for me," Jiro answered in a voice a couple of octaves lower than normal.

"Ready for a rematch? Or should I say, are you ready to lose again?" Alice taunted.

"Oh, you're so going down."

"Let's do this."

That was Kiku's cue to move. She picked up her bag and sprinted down the hall. As she approached a security camera, she couldn't help glancing up at the lens, though she knew Alice was performing a rolling blackout as Kiku moved through the building.

She climbed the sixteen stories to the roof, her legs pumping like pistons. By the time she reached the access door, her thighs felt like they were on fire, and so did her lungs. It would have been worse if she hadn't trained in the hotel room to run with the parachute pack.

With shaking hands she picked the lock, then heaved open the heavy door, dropped the gear bag on the roof, and pulled out Hwan's high-tech lockout device. It was designed to secure doors during evictions, but this one could be operated remotely. After attaching the device to the roof access door, she ran to the west railing and clamped on the winches. When they were ready, she checked her harness, goggles, and gun. Everything was good to go.

"In place," she said.

Alice and Alex were just finishing their first match with Jiro. It was clear from the trash-talking that Jiro had won.

"No way," Alice said. "This next match is mine."

Kiku grabbed the two lines and climbed over the railing. The lights of the city glimmered beneath her as she rappelled down the side of the building, past the two floors of office space, and silently dropped onto Jiro's balcony. Inside his dimly lit room, Jiro was busy playing and had thick earphones on.

Kiku pulled enough slack in both ropes so she could easily reach him. One rope was attached to her harness, the other to a rescue lasso used to save drowning victims.

The balcony slider made only a squeak as Kiku opened it. No one ever seemed to lock their balcony door, and it was a foolish mistake. Kiku slipped inside. Silently, she crossed the room and pressed the barrel of her gun against the back of Jiro's head.

Calmly removing his headphones, she said softly in his ear—the one without a hearing aid, "Lean forward and raise your hands."

"Kiku, p-please—" Jiro stuttered.

"Shut up, do everything I say, and you will live."

Jiro leaned forward and raised his hands. Kiku slipped the rescue harness over his arms and cinched it tightly around his chest.

The door to his bedroom opened. “We’re ordering a pizza. Do you want—”

Before the guard could draw his weapon, Kiku shot him. She pressed the button on Jiro’s winch and the rope tightened, yanking Jiro back in the chair and tipping it over. Like a fish getting reeled into a boat, Jiro flailed around as he was dragged across the floor and out to the balcony, his feet disappearing from sight.

Kiku followed, her pistol trained on the door. There was shouting now.

“Kiku!” Alice’s voice was frantic. “Get out of there!”

Another guard, gun in hand, appeared in the doorway. Kiku dropped him with three shots, then stepped onto the balcony and clicked the button for her own winch. The rope attached to her harness went taut, and she started to climb.

She quickly caught up to Jiro, who merely hung there, twenty feet below the roof, the winch above him making a grinding sound. It had jammed and would lift him no further. He would have to climb the rest of the way on his own.

“Climb!” Kiku ordered.

“I can’t. I can’t.” Jiro looked close to tears. He stared, wild-eyed, at the ground below.

Cursing, Kiku pulled herself up and onto the roof. Someone was already pounding on the roof access door. She planted her feet and tried to pull Jiro up.

“I’m ready,” Hwan said.

“Not yet!” Kiku snapped.

“Kiku …” Alice’s voice was tense but even. “There are ten men coming up to the roof. They are all armed. Some have machine guns.”

“Jiro is stuck twenty feet down.” Kiku tried restarting the winch. The motor whined and died.

“Kiku, get out of there,” Alice pleaded. “Leave him and go.”

Kiku looked around and spotted a large air-conditioning unit. She dashed over to it and pulled open the access panel. There was just enough space for her to fit inside, even while wearing the parachute. She squeezed herself inside and closed the panel behind her. “Hwan, unlock the roof door.”

"Kiku, no!" Alice shouted.

"There are too many," Alex added.

"Hwan, *now*!"

"Okay," Hwan said. "It's open."

Through the vents, Kiku saw the men streaming onto the roof. Nelson waved his hand, and the men started fanning out.

"You can't escape, Kiku!" Nelson shouted.

In the darkness, Kiku smiled. Nelson was a fool. She had *allowed* him and his men onto the roof for a good reason: so they couldn't escape.

"Hwan," Kiku whispered. "Lock the door. Kill the power."

Kiku closed her eyes and pulled on her night-vision goggles. Though the plan had been to use them when she BASE-jumped off the roof, they would now give her the advantage in this fight.

She opened the panel and slipped out. She had expected Hwan's device to short out the power for the block. But whatever he had done had caused a blackout across the entire city. All the better.

Two of the men turned to flee, but the door had shut behind them.

"Open the door!" one man yelled.

"It's locked!" cried the other.

Kiku watched Nelson, and saw the look on his face change. Puzzlement changed to anger, and then to fear. He had realized his mistake. He had a small army of men with him, but now he was trapped in the dark with a monster.

Kiku raced around the perimeter of the roof, shooting with a cold focus. Nelson's men panicked. Some ran. Some hid. She took them down one after the other, three shots apiece. When she reached the end of a magazine, the delay before the next shot was less than a second as she ejected the spent magazine and slapped another in its place.

Nelson had a machine gun and was randomly spraying bullets into the darkness. He killed one of his own men and wounded another before he ran out of bullets.

Kiku moved with the grace of a dancer as she whirled around the roof, slaying the men who had sought to kill her, continuing her dance of death until Nelson was the only one left.

Kiku had deliberately left him for last. Not because she was a cat playing with its prey, but because she wanted information.

Nelson had found his flashlight and he began waving it around in the hope of blinding her in the night-vision goggles. It was a poor plan.

Kiku shot him in the leg and he pitched forward, screaming in pain. The gun tumbled from his hand as he sprawled out on the roof, and the flashlight rolled to a stop, illuminating his face.

"Where is Kenzo now?" Kiku asked, raising her gun.

A shot rang out. Kiku ducked and spun toward the sound.

One of Nelson's men was still alive—though wounded by Nelson's wild machine-gunfire—and it was this man who had taken the shot. He was sitting in the darkness, clutching his stomach with one hand.

He tossed the gun away from himself and called out, "He killed my brother."

When Kiku looked back at Nelson, he was dead from a gunshot wound to the head. She sprinted to the wounded man, but he was no longer breathing.

Kiku ran back to the ropes. "Getting Jiro," she said into the mic.

"You're alive?" Alex said, with wonder in his voice.

"No chatter. Hwan, how long do I have before the power comes on?"

"It could be any time now."

Kiku grabbed her own rope and lowered it to Jiro. She cursed herself for not thinking of this before. "Grab the rope," she said.

When he had a firm hold, she winched him up onto the roof.

"Kiku, I'm—"

"Shut up until we are on the ground."

Kiku strapped him into his harness, gripped him by the shoulder, and led him over to a bank of box fans at one corner of the building. She boosted him up on top, then climbed up after and hooked his harness to hers.

Jiro shook his head in fear.

"If you scream or so much as make a peep, I will tear one of your ears off," Kiku said. "Do you understand?"

Jiro nodded.

Kiku leapt off into the darkness.

She threw her handheld deployment bag, her only option for such a low BASE jump, and a second later her chute deployed. The uncomfortable jerk upward was followed by a rush of adrenaline as they floated serenely toward the street.

Kiku took off the goggles. There was enough light to see, courtesy of the headlights of the cars below. The parachute canopy over her head had several bullet holes, but they didn't seem to be affecting its performance. Through the holes, Kiku glimpsed the stars, and she smiled.

Phase one is complete. Now comes the hard part.

32

The streetlights clicked back on just as Kiku landed close to Hwan's van. She gathered up the parachute and unhooked Jiro from her harness.

"In the back. Now." Jiro gave her a skeptical look and she snarled, "Run and I will shoot you in the leg."

As soon as she and Jiro were in the back of the van, Hwan started driving.

Kiku motioned to the floor. "Sit down, Jiro."

Jiro swayed as he remained standing, holding a handle on the inside of the van. "Go to hell."

"Eventually," Kiku said. "But is that any way to thank me? You will note that this is the second time I have rescued you."

"*Rescued* me?" Jiro growled as he finally sat down. His anger was rising. "You mean *kidnapped* me. My father will have your head on a spike."

"I am not kidnapping you, and I am not ransoming you. I rescued you because I need you to testify against Kenzo. You kept the books for him. You have enough information on his financial dealings to put him in jail for life."

Jiro looked at her like she'd just grown wings. "You want me to flip? I will never testify against my father!"

"Has anyone told you what happened in Noshiro? Or of the … situation with Daichi?"

Jiro sneered. "I have heard the lies. You lied to my father, to Takeo, and to me about my uncle's death. And Daichi tried to get under my father's skin by lying and saying he slept with my mother."

"Daichi was not lying."

"He was. And even if he was telling the truth, I would never testify against Kenzo. It would be suicide."

Kiku removed two wrinkled photographs from her tactical vest and held them out to him. "The first photo is of Kenzo and Daichi when your 'uncle' was twenty-six. The second is of Takeo when he was the same age."

Jiro's eyes widened. The resemblance was unmistakable.

"You know what Kediri, your grandfather, did when mixed-race Daichi showed up wanting to be recognized as his son. When Kenzo gets the DNA results and finds out for certain that you are Daichi's … what do you think he is going to do to you?"

"I'll testify," Jiro said without hesitation.

In the front of the van, Hwan coughed to cover his laugh. Jiro's shoulders slumped. As he closed his eyes and leaned his head back against the side of the van, a tear rolled down his cheek.

When Kiku started frisking him, he snapped, "Can you give me a minute? I'm unarmed."

Kiku backhanded him across the face. "You lost most of my sympathy when you set me up to die. When you targeted Takeo, you lost it all." She continued to pat him down until she was satisfied that he was unarmed.

"I told you I don't have a weapon," Jiro sneered, adjusting his hearing aid and pushing his glasses up his nose.

"And that is foolish. Nelson would not have hesitated to put a bullet in your head. I will take you straight to the police."

Jiro scoffed. "Not in Vegas. Do you know how many of the police here are on Kenzo's payroll? I wouldn't last a minute." He crossed his arms. "I want a good deal, and I'm not going to get it with any local yokels. Take me to DC."

"You are not in a position to make demands."

Jiro's eyes narrowed. "This is my life we're talking about." He pointed a shaking finger at her. "*And* yours. You want to get to Kenzo through me? Then you need my testimony. Which means you need me to live." His eyes widened with realization. "And I have to get my stash."

"We cannot go back to the hotel."

"I don't have it there—I'm not a fool. I never trusted my father, especially after we made the truce. I backed everything up on a hard drive."

Kiku leaned forward. "Where is it?"

"At my girlfriend's."

"We're at the car," Hwan said.

The van rolled to a stop. Kiku braced her hand against the side of the van next to Jiro's head.

"Do not make me kneecap you," she warned. Then she moved up behind Hwan. "Leave the van. There is a car rental two blocks north. Rent a car, drive up to Dry Lake, and switch cars. Head west and change cars at least two more times. Then have Daisy"—their code name for Lilly—"come and get you. Do you understand?"

Hwan shook his head. "I want to help you."

She squeezed his shoulder. "You have performed your role flawlessly. No one can help me with this next part. Go and be safe, my friend."

Hwan nodded and got out.

Kiku opened the back door, and she and Jiro jumped down. She told herself not to look back as Hwan walked away, but she still glanced over her shoulder. She was relieved when she saw that he was heading north, as she had instructed.

She pressed a button on her key fob, and a sedan down the block flashed its headlights. "Get in," she ordered as she walked to the driver's side.

When they were seated, she pulled out her phone. "Where is your girlfriend?"

He gave her an address on Dixon Street, which Kiku entered into her GPS. "Why did you not back up the files to the internet?"

"Are you kidding? My father doesn't trust the web. He thinks everyone's watching—especially the Russians. And his men actually were watching me, so I had to get creative. I backed up my laptop to an external hard drive, then I bought a teddy bear in the hotel gift shop, stuffed the hard drive inside, and shipped it to her."

Kiku pulled away from the curb. "So you do not even know if she has it?"

"She has it. I talk to her every day."

"What data is on this hard drive?"

"Everything. But I'm not going down for it. I want a great—no, an unbelievable deal. I'll bring it to the Feds and no one else."

Kiku scowled, and Jiro leaned away from her.

"Don't even think about threatening me," he said. "I've encrypted the hard drive. Unless you know the key—and no one does except me —you'll never be able to open it." He crossed his arms triumphantly.

Kiku smiled. If she wanted, she could make Jiro give her the encryption key. In fact, within ten minutes, she could make him *beg* her to take it.

"You have a new girlfriend? You seem to have gotten over Jessica quickly, considering that relationship ended with her head getting shipped to Kenzo." A little reminder of how vulnerable he was.

Jiro glared out the window. "I haven't forgotten. Jessica meant a lot to me, but we weren't exclusive. Besides, she'd want me to be happy."

A few minutes later they arrived at the address, an apartment complex with five buildings each holding maybe twenty units. Their occupants were upper middle class, judging by the cars parked outside.

"Building Two," Jiro said.

Kiku parked in a yellow-lined guest spot. "What is this new girlfriend's name?"

"Amethyst Skye."

"Interesting name. What does Miss Skye do for a living?"

"She's a model, but she's working a night job until she gets picked up by an agency. And you're not one to judge anyone's job."

Kiku shrugged. There was time enough later to ponder whether what she did was right or wrong. What mattered now was whether she was doing her job well. "After you."

Jiro led the way to the building's main entrance and rang the buzzer for number 216.

After a moment, a woman's voice answered. "Hello?"

"Hey, baby. It's me." After an awkward pause he added, "Jiro."

"Oh, hey." She coughed. "I'm kinda not feeling well. I actually called into work; I'm going to stay home."

"You know that bear I gave you? I need it back."

"What do you mean? It was a gift."

"Yeah, but I need it back. Just buzz me up." Jiro's face was turning red.

"I told you, I'm sick. It's late—come back tomorrow. And the bear's mine." She clicked off.

"Amethyst! Amethyst?" Jiro buzzed again, but she didn't answer. "Now what?"

A tall man carrying a bag of groceries approached the door. Kiku put on her friendliest smile. "Excuse me, sir, we're friends of Amethyst Skye, and we're picking her up for a movie, but she's in the shower. Would you mind letting us in?"

"Sure, that's cool." The man opened the door, and Kiku held it open so he could enter. As he walked down the hallway, Jiro started up the stairs.

"We get the bear and we go. Do not start a fight," Kiku said.

"Why would I start a fight? She's sick; I wouldn't do that."

"Because she is not sick. She is with another man."

"What? Amethyst? No way. *You're* the one starting a fight, Kiku, talking smack like that."

"You will see."

At 216, Jiro knocked softly. The door was yanked open by a huge man covered in tattoos and piercings. He glared at Jiro and held a beefy finger in his face. "You stupid or something? She said you couldn't come up."

Jiro swallowed and stepped back. "I—I just need that bear and we'll go."

Kiku raised an eyebrow. How could this coward possibly be Daichi's son? Takeo would have shot the guy in the knee by now.

"What the hell is *this*?" Amethyst shrieked, pushing her way past the big man and standing with her bare feet apart. She was in her early twenties, and wore a hot-pink pushup bra and a miniskirt unbuttoned at the waist. In her left hand was a gutted bear with stuffing falling out of it. In her right hand was the hard drive.

"You smuggled this in *my* bear?" she said, her voice rising. "You know what? Now *this* is mine too!" She held the hard drive up in the air triumphantly.

Kiku hit the man in the throat with the ridge of her left hand, then pushed his chest back and kicked his legs out from under him. He landed flat on his back so hard a stack of plates on the kitchen counter slid off and shattered on the tile floor next to him.

Kiku dragged Jiro behind her as she stepped into the apartment, slammed the door shut, and pointed her gun at Amethyst. "Shut up. Do not say another word. I already want to shoot you for being so very annoying."

Amethyst nodded like a wild-eyed bobblehead.

"Sit." Kiku pulled out a kitchen chair. "Jiro, get something to tie them up with."

Jiro rummaged around in a closet before returning with a roll of duct tape. As he taped Amethyst to the chair, Kiku took the hard drive from her hand. When Amethyst was bound and gagged, Jiro did the same to the big man.

"I'm sorry," Jiro mumbled to Amethyst.

Kiku took him by the elbow and dragged him out into the hall.

"You don't need to drag me around. I'm going," Jiro protested as she shoved him ahead of her down the stairs.

"Not fast enough," Kiku said. "If I had the time, I would slap you again. But we need to get moving."

"Why? You killed all of Kenzo's men."

"That was the B-Team watching over you. Do I really have to tell you that Kenzo has his own private security force? They are the real professionals."

"I want to hold on to that hard drive," Jiro said as they approached the front door.

Kiku grabbed him, spun him around, and slammed him against the tenant mailboxes. "Listen to me, Jiro. Talk when I say talk. Open your mouth again—"

A red dot appeared on the side of Jiro's head.

Kiku yanked Jiro down to the floor as a hail of bullets tore through the glass beside the front door. She pulled out her pistol, fired five quick shots out into the darkness, and started dragging Jiro backward.

When they were around the corner, Kiku pulled him to his feet.

"Who are those guys?" Jiro asked.

"That would be the A-Team."

Kiku pushed him down the hallway and they both took off running.

33

Jiro started to run for the side exit, but Kiku reeled him in and kept hold of his arm while she pounded on the door of an apartment at the back of the building.

A middle-aged man cautiously opened the door.

"My ex-boyfriend is out front and he has a gun," Kiku said, pushing past the man and pulling Jiro after her. "Please call the police."

Every little bit helps. If officers were alerted that a woman and man were on the run, it would work to their advantage to look like they were the good guys. Ignoring the stunned man's protests, they ran through the apartment and left through the sliding door to a small parking lot. Between them and the next apartment building it was clear.

"Run," Kiku ordered.

Jiro, out of shape from his lifestyle of gambling, womanizing, and playing video games, huffed and panted beside her. Bullets churned up the turf at their feet just as they reached cover, and though he continued wheezing and gasping, Jiro sped up at the last minute.

They ducked behind the privacy fencing and sprinted past all the apartments in the next building, keeping low. When they reached the end, Jiro doubled over and threw up.

Kiku peeked around the corner to scan the parking lot. A man and his girlfriend were getting out of a new Mustang GT. Kiku grabbed Jiro by his shirt collar and pulled him toward the car.

"Help! My boyfriend can't breathe. He's allergic to peanuts."

The man rushed over while his girlfriend pulled out her phone. Once the man was close, Kiku pointed her gun at his chest. "Keys. Now."

The man went pale, but he clutched the keys in his hand.

"You have insurance." Kiku raised the gun slightly.

"I just got her," he said, glancing lovingly at the Mustang.

"Is she worth your girlfriend's life?" Kiku aimed her pistol at the sweet-faced young woman. It was only a bluff, but he didn't know that.

The man hesitated. The girlfriend gasped and scowled at him.

Kiku aimed at the man's crotch. "Keys."

Eyes wide, he tossed her the keys, while his soon-to-be-former girlfriend dashed away.

"Go after her, you dullard," Kiku advised.

Headlights were sweeping the parking lot and men were shouting as Kiku pushed Jiro toward the passenger side and climbed behind the wheel. She started the Mustang and dropped it into reverse just as a dark sedan pulled into the parking lot behind them. The sedan rocketed forward, the driver expecting Kiku to change course and drive forward as well, but Kiku kept the car in reverse and stomped on the gas. As the two vehicles passed each other, Kiku fired several shots into the other car.

The sedan swerved wildly and slammed into a parked car. Kiku jammed on the brakes and cut the wheel. The car swung around almost one hundred eighty degrees, then Kiku dropped it into drive and pushed the gas pedal to the floor.

Jiro pulled on his seat belt and death-gripped the grab handle above his head, while the Mustang sped around the corner toward the front entrance. Three sedans blocked the exit in a formation typically used by the police for a roadblock: two cars facing each other with the third parked slightly behind and in the middle. Even in a bigger car, Kiku wouldn't be able to ram her way out. But her superior speed was her ally here.

A white SUV jumped and bucked as it flew over the speed bumps trying to block off her escape. Kiku kept the gas down and turned left, cutting between the gym and pool buildings.

"This is not a road!" Jiro yelled.

The tires threw pea gravel into the air as Kiku navigated the zero-water landscaping. They hit the artificial grass and slid. It was like driving on a frozen pond, and Kiku used minor corrections of the steering wheel as she goosed the gas to keep them heading straight.

The SUV barreled after them, and the men blocking the exit jumped into their cars. Kiku steered toward the upcoming building. The only route was right along the back of the building, through the individual backyards, which were separated from one another by privacy fencing. Kiku prayed she could bust through the wide panels in the fencing and avoid the fence posts.

"Fence! Fence!" Jiro shouted.

The Mustang's front bumper plowed through the vinyl fencing, sending PVC shards into the air. Kiku steered carefully as she struck each panel in the chain, carefully avoiding the apartments' two-foot-high cement patios just off to one side.

The SUV driver was attempting to follow, and it did not end well for them. Perhaps the driver didn't see the patios because of the fence pieces lying on the ground, or perhaps the SUV was just too hard to control on the slick turf. But the SUV's front tire slammed into a cement slab and the vehicle's entire front end bounced high into the air like a rearing horse, its spinning front tires clawing the air. When it crashed back to the ground, it landed halfway on the side of the patio, rolled over onto its roof, and finally stopped moving.

Kiku steered across another patch of grass, fighting to keep the car on course. Police sirens sounded in the distance.

Jiro looked behind them and cheered. "That was awe—"

His compliment ended in a grunt when the Mustang jerked sideways from the slam into its back quarter panel on the passenger side. The rear window cracked, and Kiku and Jiro flopped to the left like rag dolls.

Kiku pressed down the gas as the Mustang scraped along the side of the sedan. "Get down."

nearest car. She leaned him against the passenger side, then crossed to the driver's side, smashed the window with the butt of her gun, and hotwired the car.

Taking back roads toward the interstate, Kiku kept an eye out for more police, but after two cruisers flew past her in the opposite direction, she saw no more. Still, it would be best to switch vehicles again. She needed to drop out of sight.

And more importantly, she needed to know how Kenzo's men had known where to find her.

34

About an hour later, Kiku and Jiro crossed the state line into Arizona. They'd lost some time but gained some peace of mind by switching vehicles twice—stealing one at a rest stop where they paused to clean themselves up, and another from a strip mall—and Kiku intended to get another vehicle before long. But first, they needed to rest. Her head was pounding, and Jiro didn't look too good.

She pulled off the highway and parked the car outside a restaurant surrounded by four national chain hotels. Twenty minutes later they were checked into a nondescript room on the second floor. Kiku would have preferred the ground floor, but it was an easy drop from the balcony to the ground.

"I'll testify in DC," Jiro reassured her as he flopped into a chair. "But I'll need serious witness protection. Can you make that happen?"

Kiku sat down on one of the two beds. "I have a friend with contacts. I will arrange it."

They sat in silence for several moments before Jiro spoke again. "Is my brother alive?"

Kiku's eyes narrowed. "Do not speak of Takeo."

"I didn't *want* him dead, I just ..."

Kiku placed her hands in her lap instead of where she wanted to put them—around Jiro's throat. "Your plan was brilliant. How you ever came up with it is beyond me."

Jiro scowled. "See? That's exactly why I did it. You. Takeo. My father. All of you always looking down your nose at me. I wanted to show you that I could lead. And I did."

"No, you *failed*. And for what?" Kiku's head throbbed. "You were the pampered son of a mobster with a gift for finance. You had everything you needed, and you should have been happy with that. Instead, you wanted more. You are like a singer who wants to be a movie star. Sometimes you should just shut up and sing."

"My plan would have worked if it wasn't for you."

Kiku inhaled slowly. "When the Russians first kidnapped you, you were at that nightclub to try to make a deal with them, correct?"

"Yeah. They double-crossed me."

Kiku shook her head. "Of course they did."

"See! You always look at me like I'm something you just scraped off the bottom of your shoe."

"Because you are a fool."

Jiro rubbed his right thumb across the back of his left hand. "Is Takeo alive?"

"Ask me a third time and you will have to write down your answers to the Feds."

Jiro glared at her and stood. "I'm taking a quick shower." He limped into the bathroom.

Kiku walked to the balcony and took out her phone to call the one man who could help her now.

"Hello, Jack."

"Nice to hear your voice, Kiku. Alice has been really, really quiet lately whenever I ask her about you. You're not getting my future wife involved in things that she shouldn't be, are you?" There was some mirth in Jack's tone, but she knew he was serious.

"I apologize, but I need your help."

"What can I do?"

Kiku smiled. Jack was ever the white knight. She could picture him scooping up his keys, ready to rush out and slay the dragon.

"I have a bit of a situation."

Kiku told Jack about Jiro, the information he had, and what she wanted to do.

"I worked a Mafia case a while back," Jack said, "involving the daughter of a mob boss. I made some trusted contacts in witness protection. I can arrange a meeting."

"Given my position, I would prefer to hand Jiro over to you and for you to make the exchange. I need to remain invisible. But I cannot stress enough the danger this would put you in. If you decline, I understand."

"I'll do it."

Kiku closed her eyes. She had known he would say yes. If there had been another way, she would not have asked him. But their paths seemed destined to intersect.

"When and where?"

"Two days," Kiku said. "I am in Arizona. I will meet you at the Madison Creek Motel in Leavells, Virginia, about an hour south of DC."

"Got it. Do you need help before then?"

"No. Thank you, Jack. For everything."

"I'll see you in two days."

As Kiku hung up, the bathroom door opened. A wet-haired Jiro walked out, putting his hearing aid back in. "Your turn in the shower," he said.

"I am going to have a cup of tea first." Kiku held up a single tea bag encased in cellophane. "If you can call it that. Would you care for one?"

"No." Jiro flopped into a chair. "But thanks."

Kiku nodded.

"What's going to happen to me?"

"I suspect that for the next three years you will be shuttled around and raked over the coals while you are grilled about all of Kenzo's dealings."

"Not that. Now. What happens now?"

"We will meet a friend of mine in two days in Leavells, Virginia, just outside of DC."

"I'm only going to talk to the Feds."

"He is arranging it."

"Who is this friend?"

35

Kiku drove with hardly a break for the next two days, stopping only to rest briefly at no-tell motels. But every mile they traveled, the nagging feeling that something terrible was on the horizon grew stronger.

Still, in spite of worry and sleep deprivation, she felt relieved and wide awake as they neared Leavells. She would hand Jiro over to Jack. She would follow them both to DC, stick around until the swap was made, and then disappear, refresh, and regroup.

Jiro, too, seemed relieved and eager to arrive. She guessed that he'd come to terms with his limited options and realized that incarceration was better than death. She couldn't say the same for herself—she would much prefer death.

Her phone buzzed with a text from Jack. *Almost there. Have 2 get gas.*

She replied with the thumbs-up emoji.

"Hey," Jiro said, sitting up and rubbing his eyes. "Can we get something to eat before we get there?"

"No."

"Come on." Jiro pointed at a lone diner on the side of the road. "We can grab something there."

"It is closed. It only serves breakfast and lunch." There was no way Kiku was stopping so close to their destination. "You should have asked for something earlier."

"Earlier I was sleeping," Jiro grumbled.

Kiku's phone buzzed again.

"You have a problem." Hwan's voice was tight with tension. "A big problem. The picture you sent me, of the circuit board? It took me a while to figure it out, but I'm sure now. It's not just a tracker, it's a microphone. Did you say anything aloud about where you're going?"

She had, but that wasn't foremost in her mind. She was most concerned with remembering if she'd said anything about the farm. Or Jack and Alice. Her heart thumped in her chest. She didn't *think* she had ...

But that wasn't good enough. Takeo's life might hang on what she had said. Or Alice's and Jack's.

"Thank you for warning me. I will take this into consideration."

She hung up, then mentally ran through all of the conversations she'd had with Jiro prior to discovering the tracker. They had not talked much, and as she grew more confident that she hadn't said anything to compromise her friends, her breathing grew easier.

But I told Jiro where the meet with Jack was going to be.

A cable laid across the road glittered in the light of the low-hanging sun; a snake ready to strike. Kiku jerked the wheel hard to the right and swerved into the dirt at the side of the road, sending up a huge cloud of dust. Jiro's head banged against the window as they skidded around the spike strips and back onto the road.

Immediately, three black sedans pulled out onto the road in front of them and stopped in the same roadblock formation as at Jiro's girlfriend's apartment. A dozen guns opened fire. Instantly, three bullet holes appeared in the windshield, spider-webbing the glass, but neither Kiku nor Jiro was hit.

Kiku threw the wheel to the left and spun the car one hundred eighty degrees. She stomped on the gas, her tires squealing, and took off the way she'd come.

A bullet came through the rear window and took a chunk of fluff out of the side of her headrest before making another hole in the windshield. Two more hit the headliner, and several more pinged off the back of the car. Jiro threw his hands over his head and ducked. Kiku just kept driving.

She spotted the glistening spike strip up ahead when a man with a pistol ran out of the tall grass to their right and started firing at the car. She steered right for him. The man fired twice more, then tried to dodge, but Kiku called his bluff, hitting him head-on, and the bumper lifted him up and over the car.

Not stopping, Kiku swerved back onto the road and tried to get more speed, but puffs of smoke were rising from the hood of the car. The check engine light came on and the temperature gauge rose steadily.

Kiku steeled her nerves and retraced the route they had traveled, a back road with little of note on it. The only building of any size, other than the diner, was the gas station twenty miles back. They'd never make it.

Kiku pulled out her phone and dialed Jack.

Four SUVs appeared on the road far ahead of her, taking up both lanes.

Jack answered. "Hi, Kiku, I'm ten minutes away but have to get gas—"

"Jack, I walked into an ambush," Kiku said calmly. "I am taking cover in the Daydream Diner on Route One-Four-Seven. I will hide the hard drive somewhere inside." She turned to Jiro. "The encryption key. Do not make me force you to give it to me."

Jiro's face was pale. He closed his eyes and hung his head. "If I tell you, you'll leave me to die."

Kiku ground her teeth. He was right. She *would* leave him. And without it, she couldn't afford to leave him.

Gray, oily smoke was pouring out of the engine as they approached the diner. She ran through a quick calculation in her head. Six SUVs and three sedans, each with four-man teams ... at least thirty-six attackers. There was no way she would be able to hold them off until Jack got there.

"Bring the police with you when you come. Please tell Alice I am sorry I could not attend your wedding."

"Kiku! Kiku, listen—"

Kiku hung up and aimed the car at the front doors of the diner. "Hang on."

Jiro braced himself as Kiku barreled off the road, through the parking lot, and smashed right through the diner's front entrance. The sound of breaking aluminum and shattering glass mixed with the wail of a blaring alarm.

Kiku skidded to a stop next to the breakfast counter, kicked her door open, grabbed her bag, and got out. But Jiro was having trouble. The passenger-side door was jammed against the dessert counter and wouldn't budge. So Kiku leaned in, seized him by the arm, and pulled him out on her side.

The sedans reached the diner first and skidded to a stop, forming a half circle in the dirt parking lot. They didn't see Kiku half dragging, half pushing Jiro toward a walk-in freezer. She pulled open the heavy door and shoved him inside.

"Get in the corner and stay down." She opened her bag and handed him her backup pistol. "If you do not hear a whistle before the door opens, shoot whoever steps through the doorway."

"Wait! Where are you going?" Jiro said. But Kiku was already moving.

She ducked low behind the counter as she hurried over to the fire exit. The security alarms were already blaring, so when she opened the door, setting off the fire alarm too, it barely added to the mix. She slipped past several trash cans and noted the huge propane tank as she moved to the rear corner of the building. Behind the building was nothing but a flat, open field. More dust, as far as the eye could see. She wouldn't make it fifty yards before being cut down. Escape was impossible.

She moved to the front corner and peered around it. The SUVs had just arrived. At least a dozen men jumped out, led by Ryder. Each man was armed with a pistol or shotgun, and all of them had tactical gear for war: bulletproof vests, extra magazines, flashbangs. Taking them on would be suicide; what she needed was some way of slowing them down.

A smile spread across her face as a plan came together.

Pressing herself against the wall at the corner of the building, she started firing at the closest men, dropping three before anyone managed to return fire. Then she quickly ducked back inside through the fire door. In addition to the bullets flying toward the spot she'd just vacated, other bullets were much closer, tearing through the smashed front entrance and causing damage in the kitchen. Kiku crouch-walked behind the counter, past the long line of stoves, turning each knob as she went. As she dove across the open space between the counter and the freezer, gas hissed behind her and bullets pinged off the tile and shattered dishware.

Kiku whistled and opened the freezer door. Jiro was hiding in the back corner, his gun trained on the door.

"Point that another way," Kiku ordered.

He lowered the weapon.

Kiku peered over the counter.

"Kiku!" Ryder yelled from outside the diner. He removed a flash-bang from his belt and pulled the pin. "Kenzo sends his regards."

Kiku smiled.

Ryder is so very predictable.

Kiku jumped into the freezer and slammed the door shut. "Cover your ears!" She crouched low and did the same.

Even from inside the insulated metal freezer, the explosion was deafening, and the entire structure shook, sending shelves of frozen food tumbling to the floor around them. Dust rained down from the ceiling like snow on a winter day.

"Stay here," Kiku said.

Jiro's eyes were wide. "No problem."

Kiku shook her head, blinked rapidly, and shoved the door open. A vast space stretched out before her, and the darkening sky hung above. It took her a second to realize that most of the walls and ceiling had collapsed in the explosion. She was amazed nothing was on fire, though smoke rose from several charred booths.

Outside, Ryder's men had been thrown backward by the force of the blast. They lay on their backs all around. Only a couple of them were regaining their footing, and they appeared dazed.

This was the window of opportunity she had been waiting for. She jumped the counter, ran past the mangled mess that was once the front entrance, and sprinted directly toward Ryder, who had risen to his knees. When he saw Kiku, he fumbled for his gun, but he wasn't fast enough. She dropped him with the first shot and pumped two more into him for good measure.

It was a target-rich environment. She turned from side to side, gunning down Ryder's men as she moved toward the only real cover left: the SUVs. The men who had been in the sedans or farther away from the explosion began firing back.

Bullets whizzing around her, she ducked behind a vehicle and put three rounds in each of the tires on her side. The SUV slumped to the ground, providing more protection for her lower body. But other men were now recovering from the explosion, and the spray of bullets was becoming a thick volley.

One man came around on her left, attempting to flank her. She cut him down. Another took his place, and she dropped him, too. Her magazine was empty and she swapped it out for a fresh one.

Her last one.

She pulled out the hard drive and hid it underneath the rear bumper of the SUV. Then she took out her phone and texted the location to Jack.

As she was typing it in, she heard the sirens—faint, but drawing closer. She'd spent a lifetime dreading that sound, but now it was the sweetest sound she'd ever heard.

Flying down the road toward her was a police cruiser with its lights blazing. Kiku was aware that in the United States, the police had a limit on how fast they could travel, and yet this vehicle appeared to be going at least one hundred fifty miles per hour.

Her white knight had arrived.

Kiku fired three more rounds.

The police cruiser skidded into the parking lot. A huge dust cloud washed over her, temporarily obscuring her from Ryder's men.

The car door opened and Jack Stratton dashed through the haze. Six foot one, fit, and handsome as ever, he tossed her a combat shotgun, hefted an assault rifle of his own, and began firing at Ryder and his men.

"You have impeccable timing," Kiku said. She raised the shotgun and cut down a man trying to use the cover of the dust cloud to rush their position. "Please tell me you brought backup."

Jack grinned roguishly and jerked his thumb back the way he had come. In the dusty distance she saw more than a dozen cruisers speeding toward them.

The remnants of Ryder's men were scattering. Those who could hopped into the other vehicles and took off. Those who couldn't lay on the ground, pleading in vain with their comrades to be taken away, too.

Kiku grabbed Jack and kissed him full on the lips. He squirmed and tried to pull away, but she held on to his cheeks. Finally, she let him go.

"My apologies to Alice," she said with a smile. "The hard drive is under the bumper of the car. Jiro has the encryption key."

"Where is he?"

"In the walk-in freezer."

Jack rolled his big brown eyes. "Is he breathing?"

Kiku laughed and kissed him again. "My apologies to Alice again."

Jack blushed. "Will you please stop kissing me?"

"I am sorry. But I do not know if I have ever been so happy to see a police officer. And remember, you are not married yet."

"Yeah, but if Alice finds out about you kissing me, I might never be."

"Yes, you will. My best wishes to both of you. And congratulations on getting back onto the force."

He looked puzzled. "I'm not."

"But you are driving a police car?"

"Yeah ..." Jack rubbed the back of his neck. "When you called, I was just pulling into a gas station—the Charger was down to fumes. It would have taken too long to fill up—or to explain to the cops inside getting coffee. So ..."

"You stole their police car?"

When Jack nodded, she saw that his mop of thick, dark hair was longer than she had ever seen it.

Kiku leaned in for another kiss, but Jack held her back. "If you kiss me a third time, Alice *will* murder me."

The police cruisers skidded to a stop in front of the diner.

Kiku laughed. "If there is any trouble, I will straighten it all out with Alice when I see you at the wedding. And please accept my apology to you."

"Apology to me? Why would you be apologizing to me?"

"Because of this." Kiku leapt to her feet and screamed, "Help! Help me!" She raised her hands above her head and ran toward the officers, who jumped out of their cars and pointed their guns at Jack. "Don't shoot him!" Kiku shrieked.

Jack raised his hands in surrender as half a dozen policemen closed in on him.

I'll have to get Jack and Alice a very expensive wedding gift.

36

Jack sat handcuffed in the back of the police car waiting for his friend Dan Haney to finish speaking with the sheriff. Dan was currently the assistant director of the witness protection program and might be able to dig Jack out of the hole he now found himself in.

Another unmarked federal vehicle arrived, and its two occupants walked over to the sheriff and Dan. Judging by the raised voices and index fingers stabbing in his direction, Jack had little doubt he was the subject of the conversation.

Finally, Dan smiled, shook the sheriff's hand, and walked over to Jack. "You're as reckless and crazy as ever," he said, opening the cruiser's back door.

"I didn't have a choice. You explained that, right? Do you want me to talk to them?"

"No. And yes, I explained it. More importantly, I invited the sheriff to share in the apprehension of a viper's nest of Yakuza members and mercenaries."

"So they're letting me go?"

"That's what they're currently discussing."

Jack frowned. "What's to debate? Jiro is giving them enough to take down the Yakuza."

One of the newer arrivals, a man in a dark-blue suit, came over and joined them. "What exactly are you giving us, Mr. Stratton?" he asked.

"Jack," said Dan, "this is Deputy Director Tom Walsh."

Jack got out of the car awkwardly, his hands still cuffed behind his back. "If it wasn't for me," he said, "you wouldn't have Jiro."

Tom cocked his head to the side and gave a lazy shrug. "Have you ever heard the expression, 'What have you done for me lately'? We have Jiro now. Is there something *else* you have to offer?"

Jack shook his head. The political part of police work had always bothered him. It looked like these guys were about to hang him out to dry.

He shot back, "Have *you* ever heard the saying, 'Don't count your chickens if you're a jerk'?"

Dan's eyes widened.

Jack gave him a crooked grin. "Jiro is nothing to you without his files. And I have the hard drive that contains those files."

Tom looked at Dan, who shrugged. "I didn't know about this."

"If you want what's on that hard drive, have the sheriff retroactively deputize me," Jack said. "You guys can say I was helping but the *official* paperwork hadn't come through yet."

Tom frowned, then walked over to the man he'd arrived with. The two men spoke in hushed tones for a few minutes before Tom walked back over to Jack.

"Where is the hard drive?"

Jack scoffed. "Promise me that deal and you can have it."

Tom's eyes narrowed. "There was a woman here. Do you know her?"

Jack shook his head. "Nope. Never saw her before. I can't even remember what she looked like."

Tom waved the sheriff over. "Sheriff, where is the woman who was here when your officers arrived?"

"The ambulance took her to Mercy General. She was in shock."

"Call them and tell them to bring her back here." Tom grinned smugly at Jack. "There must be some connection. I bet she's the one who brought Jiro here. They were meeting you here, Stratton. She'll know where the hard drive is."

The sheriff stepped away and spoke into his radio. After a moment his eyes bulged out and he swore.

"What did they say?" Tom snapped.

The sheriff came back, shaking his head. "You're not going to believe this, but that lady carjacked the ambulance. She tied up the crew and left them on the side of the road."

"Put out an APB on that ambulance," Tom ordered.

Jack grinned. "Looks like you need me after all. Do we have a deal?"

After a long silence, and with clenched jaw, Tom nodded.

37

"Red with white trim," Daichi said, rolling his wheelchair over to Kiku. "Custom job?"

Kiku nodded and gave her new Mercedes-Benz convertible a little pat.

"A present to myself. A chrysanthemum."

Daichi didn't smile. For a moment they both looked out across the farm, breathing the sunshine in. Finally, he broke the silence. "Kenzo is still out there. You don't have to leave."

"The snake has gone underground. Authorities the world over are hunting him. I am the least of his worries." Kiku forced herself to sound like she believed this, though she knew it to be a lie. Daichi and the others had a chance of a normal life, but Kenzo would never rest until Kiku was dead. She was certain of that.

"Takeo needs you," Daichi said. "He plans to build a legitimate Yakuza."

"I am unsure of that. Even if he starts over, the cycle repeats. Yakuza, mafia ... most gangs start with the same goal of protection, but the money corrupts. And one bad apple can spoil the whole bushel. My wish for Takeo is for him to use that brilliant mind for business and begin one of his own. If his father can put the Yakuza in the past, he can too."

Daichi flashed a grin. "Wouldn't that be nice? I thought you were taking Takeo to your friend's wedding."

"I am. But that is not for two weeks. I need to take care of something first."

"You need some down time." Daichi held out a beer.

Kiku shook her head. What she wouldn't give for a long soak in a tub with a good book and a bottle of wine. But now wasn't the time. She'd already been forced to delay too long in her hunt for the men who'd killed her sister. Kiku wouldn't make Akari wait for vengeance any longer than she had to.

And she had a lead. A name. Jeff Klein. It was Klein who had arranged the meeting at which Akari was killed. He would know who was present.

"Well, the others are staying," Daichi said, rolling his eyes. He took another sip of beer. "Hwan's already planning an addition to the house."

Kiku raised an eyebrow. "*All* the others? Even Takeo?"

Daichi nodded. "For now. Your friend Alice walked Hwan through setting up a computer that can't be traced. Takeo said he can keep things together from here while the investigations are going on."

Kiku smiled. "Who knows? Maybe after a couple more weeks of this"—she held her hand out to the sunlit fields—"Takeo will not want to leave."

"You're always welcome to stay."

Kiku leaned over and kissed Daichi's cheek. "And if I keep listening to you, I will be tempted." She stood tall and bowed low. "I am forever in your debt."

Before he could reply, she got in the car and drove away.

The front door of the farmhouse banged open, and Takeo ran stiffly out onto the porch. She watched him in the rearview mirror for only a moment before she rounded the corner. She wanted to turn around and drive back to him. She yearned to hold him, kiss him from head to toe, and make love until the stars appeared in the sky, but she wouldn't allow herself to. Not now. She had work to do.

Rocks pinged off the undercarriage of the car and dust kicked up along the sides. She drove it hard. She loved her new vehicle, but as she skidded out onto the road, she reminded herself that it was a tool created for a purpose. If she had to, she'd push the car beyond its limits and drive it into the ground.

Kiku lifted up the chrysanthemum locket on her chest and tucked it into her shirt. She, too, was created for a purpose. It was Daichi who had given her the name Kiku, but she became that new person on the day her sister died. Her little-girl self was murdered that day. She was now an *onryō*, a vengeful spirit, and she wouldn't rest until her sister was avenged.

As she sped down the road, she imagined she heard her sister's voice in the whispers of the wind: *Stop, Akiri.*

Kiku's throat tightened. Akiri. She fought to drown out the sound of her real name. She could still remember her mother calling that name as she stood in the doorway, or her father saying it softly before he kissed her goodnight.

But Akiri was her name no more.

She jammed the gas pedal to the floor and sped toward the highway.

Now, there was only Kiku.

EPILOGUE

Jeff Klein's black Town Car pulled over to the curb in front of the little stucco massage parlor. Omar Abadi, Klein's head of security, waited at the front, his highly polished shoes shining in the sun.

The chauffeur came around and opened Klein's door, and the unbearable heat of the southwest Florida sun swept the cool air-conditioning away. Klein felt a bead of sweat roll down the side of his pudgy face as he strode over to Abadi.

Abadi stood at attention, holding the door open; his crisp gray suit skimmed over his bulging muscles beneath. "All clear," he reported.

"It is ridiculous we have to go to these lengths," Klein grumbled and tugged at his shirt. He had taken to wearing boxy, Cuban-collared shirts with his expanding waistline.

"A sweep was warranted, sir."

Klein resisted the urge to tell the six-foot-five former Mossad agent that he wasn't asking for his opinion. Of course surveillance sweeps were needed. The last thing Klein needed was for someone to dig up dirt on him.

Klein stepped inside, and he was once again nestled in artificial cold. The scent of jasmine reached his nose.

"Mr. Klein." The Asian hostess, in a pale-green linen tunic and slacks, stepped forward and bowed low. "So nice to see you again."

Klein gave the older woman only a slight nod. She might have been a looker twenty years ago, but he hadn't driven all the way here to see an old broad. Southwest Florida had more old ladies than flamingos, and today he wanted to spend time with someone young, fresh.

"Is the room ready?" he asked, setting the sealed envelope down on the counter.

"Yes, Mr. Klein. It is all set. Thank you so much." She held open the curtain to the hallway.

Klein started forward, and Abadi started to follow.

"Wait here," Klein groused. This was the one time he'd get to relax all week, and he didn't want it screwed up by that lummox standing in the corner of the room the whole time.

His man frowned but kept his mouth shut.

Klein walked down the tiled hall. The last door was slightly ajar. The soft sound of wood chimes and the flicker of candles beckoned him forward.

A strikingly beautiful Asian woman appeared in the doorway. She was dressed in simple white pants and an ivory blouse, but her supple curves were evident, and she moved with a grace that reminded Klein of a ballerina on a music box. She held the door open and bowed her head.

Klein smiled widely as he strode into the small room with a long massage table and unbuttoned his shirt. He'd given up his false modesty long ago and now undressed in the presence of the masseuses. They both knew how it would end. He kicked off his loafers, removed his pants, and lay down on the massage table. Today was going to be a very good day indeed.

The woman shut and locked the door, then walked to the table and bowed. "Is the room comfortable for you?" Her voice was as soft as the sheets on the table.

"Great. Now shut off the annoying ping-ping music crap. My lower back is killing me. Don't use too much oil."

The woman pressed a button, and the wood chimes stopped their soft beat. She bowed once more. "Will there be anything else before I start?"

Klein jerked his thumb toward the ceiling. "Shut that light off. And blow the candles out."

The woman's brows knitted together.

Klein's heartbeat ticked up. He loved this part. It was a little game he played. Cat and mouse. The girls always got nervous when he asked them to shut the lights off, and that was part of the fun.

"I came here to relax," he said, "and I can't do that with the lights on."

"How am I going to see?"

Klein rolled onto his side and grabbed the woman's arm. Her skin was soft, but the muscles underneath rippled. "Feel your way around," he said with a smile.

The woman didn't try to pull away. He expected to feel a tremble, but her arm was rock solid.

"As you wish." She reached over and flipped the light switch, and the room was plunged into darkness except for the three candles, which still flickered.

Klein pulled her closer. "Are you afraid of the dark?"

"No." The candlelight reflected off the metal pin holding her hair up in a bun.

Klein let go of her arm and remained on his side, watching her. There was something different about this woman.

She leaned down and blew out one of the candles, and her hair breathed a scent of some intoxicating perfume toward him.

"Most people have a fear of the dark." Klein let his voice drop lower. He realized what bothered him about this woman: she wasn't afraid. He didn't care for that. Not at all.

"What is there to be afraid of?" She blew out the second candle. The faintest hint of a smile broke across her lips.

"When you were a child, didn't you believe that monsters live in the dark?"

The woman's canines sparkled in the light of the last candle. "Yes, I did. And it is true."

She licked her thumb and forefinger, then reached out toward the candle flame.

Klein was transfixed by the flames dancing in her black eyes. He searched for an emotion reflected there, but found nothing. Her eyes were an abyss.

He swallowed. His mouth had suddenly gone dry.

"One more thing." Her thumb and forefinger hovered on either side of the last flame. "I failed to introduce myself."

She closed her fingers, and the room was plunged into darkness.

"My name is Kiku."

JOIN THE FREE PREFERRED READER PROGRAM

Join the Preferred Reader program and get your *exclusive* copy of *FIRST PATROL*

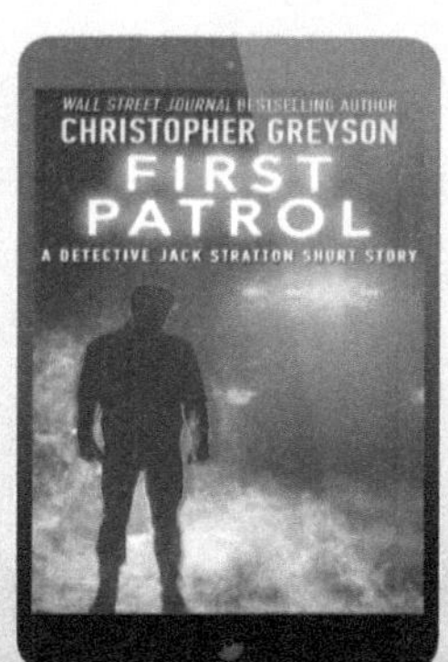

Preferred readers enjoy:

- Advanced Notification of New Book Releases
- The Christopher Greyson Newsletter
- Special Appreciation Giveaways
- The exclusive short story: FIRST PATROL!

Visit ChristopherGreyson.com to sign-up!

KIKU - YAKUZA ASSASSIN

ACTION-THRILLER NOVELS

Award-winning, *Wall Street Journal* bestselling author Christopher Greyson breaks the mold for action-thrillers. Join Kiku as she criss-crosses the globe from Chicago to Hong Kong, the streets of Japan, and the frozen tundra of Russia and takes on the mob, Yakuza, black market, and anyone else who stands in her way!

A BEAUTIFUL PLACE TO DIE

Protector. Lover. Assassin. — *Kiku.*

Orphaned as a child and taken in by the Yakuza, Kiku swore an oath to serve and protect the organization. But, when Kiku discovers that the 13-year-old boy she has been assigned to guard may be the son of her lover and heir to the Yakuza throne, her pledge is put to the test. With a price on the boy's head and a target on his back, Kiku must not only save him from the ruthless Russian mob but possibly from a traitor in the Yakuza itself. Torn between love and honor, Kiku must snatch the boy from the crosshairs before it's too late.

KINDLE THE FIRES OF WAR

She's outnumbered 100 to 1.
They're going to need more men.

Kiku has gone rogue. Now hunted by the Russian mob and the Yakuza, Kiku heads to Hong Kong's underbelly to rescue her lover. Faced with impossible odds, Kiku must outwit, outfight, and outrun everyone trying to capture her and collect the two-million-dollar bounty. Rats fueled by greed or vengeance, driven by ruthless leaders, run rampant, all hoping to score. The mob, Yakuza, and Hong Kong's black market—they all wanted to fight. Kiku started a war.

DANCE OF DEATH

To save the one she loves,
she'll kill them all.

Kiku's quest to rescue her lover has gone disastrously wrong. With the odds stacked against her, her enemies think she'll run and hide to save herself. They're wrong—dead wrong. Kiku decides to take the fight to them instead. Now the hunter, Kiku, will stop at nothing to protect those she loves.

ALSO BY
CHRISTOPHER GREYSON

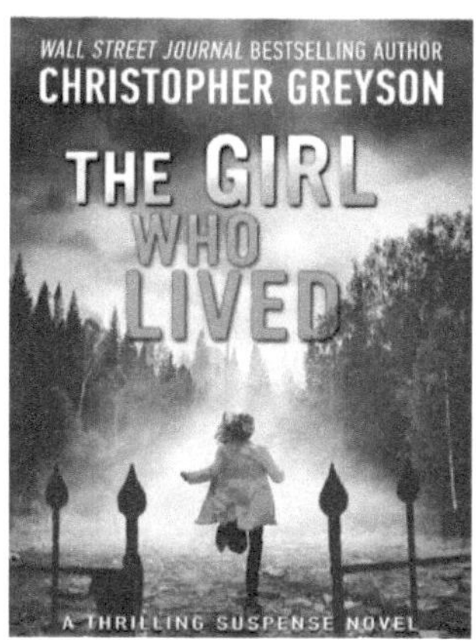

THE GIRL WHO LIVED

Ten years ago, four people were brutally murdered. One girl lived. As the anniversary of the murders approaches, Faith Winters is released from the psychiatric hospital and yanked back to the last spot on earth she wants to be—her hometown where the slayings took place. Wracked by the lingering echoes of survivor's guilt, Faith spirals into a black hole of alcoholism and wanton self-destruction. Finding no solace at the bottom of a bottle, Faith decides to track down her sister's killer—and then discovers that she's the one being hunted.

ONE LITTLE LIE

A LIE IS A WELCOME MAT FOR THE DEVIL...

Kate had high hopes when she moved to her husband‘s hometown, but her domestic bliss was short-lived. Blindsided by her spouse's public affair with his high school sweetheart, everything she worked for begins to unravel, along with her sanity. Confused, alone, and afraid, can Kate untangle the web of lies and unmask her stalker, or will she lose everything—including her life?

One Little Lie is a riveting suspense novel set in an idyllic town where money talks, gossip flows, and the court of public opinion rules. Jump on for a fun, fast-paced ride with a book you can't put down!

The Detective Jack Stratton Mystery-Thriller Series

The Detective Jack Stratton Mystery-Thriller Series, authored by *Wall Street Journal* bestselling writer Christopher Greyson, has 5,000+ five-star reviews and over a million readers and counting. If you'd love to read another page-turning thriller with mystery, humor, and a dash of romance, pick up the next book in the highly acclaimed series today:

And Then She Was GONE

A hometown hero with a heart of gold, Jack Stratton was raised in a whorehouse by his prostitute mother. When his foster mother asks him to look into a missing girl's disappearance, Jack quickly gets drawn into a baffling mystery. As Jack digs deeper, everyone becomes a suspect—including himself.

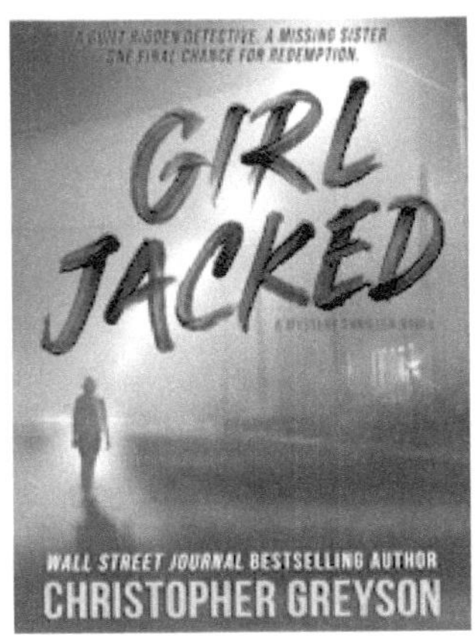

GIRL JACKED

They say a dangerous man is the one who had it all and lost it. But they're wrong, it's the one who lost everything but has a chance to get it back...

Guilt has driven a wedge between Jack and the family he loves. When Jack, now a police officer, hears the news that his foster sister Michelle is missing, it cuts straight to his core. The police think she just took off, but Jack knows Michelle would never leave her loved ones behind—like he did. Forced to confront the demons from his past, Jack must take action, find Michelle, and bring her home... or die trying.

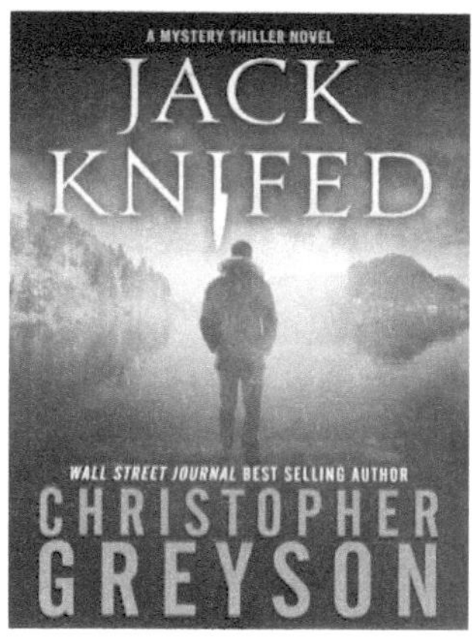

JACK KNIFED

How far would you go to uncover the truth of your past?

Constant nightmares have forced Jack to seek answers about his rough childhood and the dark secrets hidden there. The mystery surrounding Jack's birth father leads Jack to investigate the twenty-seven-year-old murder case in Hope Falls.

A heart-rending mystery-thriller about lost love, betrayal, and murder that will keep you on the edge of your seat.

JACKS ARE WILD

As the body count rises, the stakes are life and death—with no rules except one—Jacks are Wild.

When Jack's sexy old flame disappears, no one thinks it's suspicious except Jack and one unbalanced witness. Jack feels in his gut that something is wrong. He knows that Marisa has a past, and if it ever caught up with her—it would be deadly. The trail leads him into all sorts of trouble—landing him smack in the middle of an all-out mob war between the Italian Mafia and the Japanese Yakuza.

A strong hero, smart women sleuths, and more twists and turns than a piece of licorice.

JACK AND THE GIANT KILLER

A serial killer is stalking Jack's town--and no one's safe. But they don't know Jack.

Rogue hero Jack Stratton is back in another action-packed, thrilling adventure. While recovering from a gunshot wound, Jack gets a seemingly harmless private investigation job—locate the owner of a lost dog—Jack begrudgingly assists. Little does he know it will place him directly in the crosshairs of a merciless serial killer.

An action-packed thrill ride until the very end!

DATA JACK

Can Jack and Alice stop a pack of ruthless criminals before they can Data Jack?

Jack Stratton's back is up against the wall. He's broke, kicked off the force, and his new bounty hunting business has slowed to a trickle. He thinks things are turning around when Alice gets a lucrative job setting up a home data network.When the computer program the CEO invented becomes the key tool in an international data heist, things turn deadly. In this digital age of hackers, spyware, and cyber terrorism--data is more valuable than gold. The thieves plan to steal the keys to the digital kingdom and with this much money at stake, they'll kill for it. Can Jack and Alice stop the pack of ruthless criminals before they can *Data Jack*?

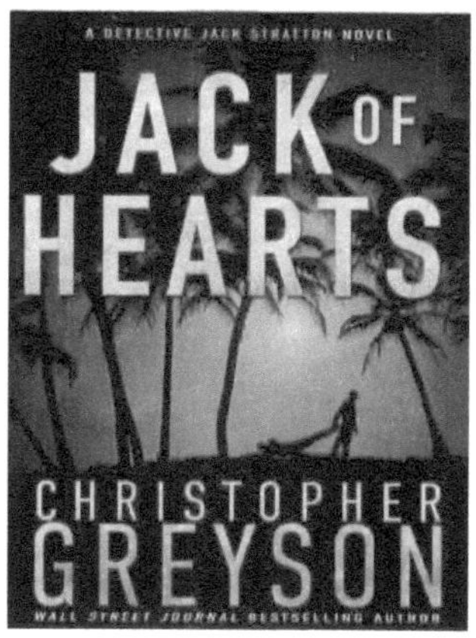

JACK OF HEARTS

Jack Stratton is heading south for some fun in the sun. Already nervous about introducing his girlfriend, Alice, to his parents, the last thing Jack needed was for the dog-sitter to cancel, forcing him to bring Lady, their 120-pound King Shepherd, on the plane with them. The dog holds Jack responsible and wants payback. On top of everything, Jack is still waiting for Alice's answer to his marriage proposal.

When his mother and the members of her neighborhood book club ask him to catch the "Orange Blossom Cove Bandit," a small-time thief who's stealing garden gnomes and peace of mind from their quiet retirement community, how can Jack refuse?

JACK FROST

What do you get when you mix the blockbuster television show Survivor with Agatha Christie's masterpiece And Then There Were None...

Jack has a new assignment: to investigate the suspicious death of a soundman on the hit TV show *Planet Survival*. Jack goes undercover as a security agent where the show is filming on nearby Mount Minuit. Soon trapped on the treacherous peak by a blizzard, a mysterious killer continues to stalk the cast and crew of *Planet Survival*. What started out as a game is now a deadly competition for survival. As the temperature drops and the body count rises, what will get them first? The mountain or the killer?

JACK OF DIAMONDS

All Jack Stratton wants to do is get married to the woman he loves—and make it through the wedding. It seems like he is finally getting his wish until he responds to a police distress call and discovers his old partner unconscious in an abandoned house. Investigators insist it was just an accident, but Jack fears there may be more to it. Sketches of women cover the walls, and among them is one sketch that makes Jack's blood run cold—a sketch of Alice, pinned up beside an invitation to a very special wedding—his own.

This time, "till death do us part"
might just be a bit too accurate!

CAPTAIN JACK

Looking forward to some fun in the surf and sand, newlyweds Jack and Alice Stratton are determined not to let something like a hurricane upset their honeymoon plans. But the storm's winds and churning tides unearthed a secret long hidden beneath the turquoise waters of the island paradise.

A local tour boat captain discovers a lost submarine and offers to sell the location to a man known only as the Dyab—the Devil. When the captain is murdered, the police suspect Jack and Alice and confiscate their passports. Trapped between the Devil and the deep blue sea, the handsome young detective and his blushing bride have nowhere to turn and everything to lose as they set out to prove their innocence and find the real killer.

Hear your favorite characters
come to life in audio versions of
the Detective Jack Stratton
Mystery-Thriller Series!
Audio Books now available on Audible!
Listen Now

Novels featuring Jack Stratton in order:
AND THEN SHE WAS GONE
GIRL JACKED
JACK KNIFED
JACKS ARE WILD
JACK AND THE GIANT KILLER
DATA JACK
JACK OF HEARTS
JACK FROST
JACK OF DIAMONDS
CAPTAIN JACK

Fantasy Adventure

PURE OF HEART

Orphaned and alone, rogue-teen Dean Walker has learned how to take care of himself on the rough city streets. Unjustly wanted by the police, he takes refuge within the shadows of the city. When Dean stumbles upon an old man being mugged, he tries to help—only to discover that the victim is anything but helpless and far more than he appears. Together with three friends, he sets out on an epic quest where only the pure of heart will prevail.

You could win a brand new
HD KINDLE FIRE TABLET
when you go to
ChristopherGreyson.com
Enter as many times as you'd like.
No purchase necessary.
It's just my way of thanking my loyal readers.

THE ADVENTURES OF FINN & ANNIE — MINIMYSTERY SERIES

In these heartwarming short stories, join Finn and Annie as they investigate their way through murder, arson, theft, embezzlement, and maybe even love, seeking to distinguish between truth and lies, scammers and victims. A Mini-Mystery series that will touch your heart and leave you craving more!

ACKNOWLEDGMENTS

I would like to thank all the wonderful readers out there. It is you who make the literary world what it is today—a place of dreams filled with tales of adventure! Word of mouth is crucial for any author to succeed. If you enjoyed the novel, please consider leaving a review at Amazon, even if it is only a line or two; it would make all the difference and I would appreciate it very much.

I would also like to thank my amazing wife for standing beside me every step of the way on this journey. My thanks also go out to my two awesome kids—Laura and Christopher, my dear mother and the rest of my family. Finally, thank you to my wonderful team, Anne Cherry, Maia McViney, Michael Mishoe, Charlie Wilson of The Book Specialist, and the unbelievably helpful beta readers!

ABOUT THE AUTHOR

My name is Christopher Greyson, and I am a storyteller. Since I was a little boy, I have dreamt of what mystery was around the next corner, or what quest lay over the hill. If I couldn't find an adventure, one usually found me, and now I weave those tales into my stories.

My love for tales of mystery and adventure began with my grandfather, a decorated World War I hero. I will never forget being introduced to his friend, a WWI pilot who flew across the skies at the same time as the feared, legendary Red Baron. I love to hear from my readers. Please go to ChristopherGreyson.com and sign up for my mailing list to receive periodic updates on new book releases. Thank you for reading my novels. I hope my stories have brightened your day.

Sincerely,

The Dance of Death

Find out more about the author and upcoming books online at www.Christopher-Greyson.com.

v.2.10.22

www.ingramcontent.com/pod-product-compliance
Lightning Source LLC
Chambersburg PA
CBHW020722310726
48979CB00004B/1026

* 9 7 8 1 6 8 3 9 9 5 2 3 4 *